After the Loss

Ben was more affectionate than a lot of dads in Caboose, and even more so after Judy left. He made it a habit to squeeze and hug and pat and lift and spin. Since his death, nobody has ever hugged me so tight. Michael mostly kept his arms at his sides, or loosely draped across the back of the sofa, or fixed to the ladder of the fire truck.

I'm not done missing Ben, and now I've started up with missing Michael, too. I'm missing him elbowing me and calling me "Beanpole" and "Lightbulb." I'm missing him pressing and pressing for me to go off to college, to go someplace else. I'm missing those few hugs I did get from him, how carefully he held me and how safe he made me feel. I squeeze Stella tighter, breathe against her warm fur. I wish Phyllis would pat my knee again. I think about Hubert, the closest relative I've got anymore. I wonder if he's the hugging type and maybe he just doesn't know me well enough yet to hug. Or maybe it's me. Maybe I'm not the kind of person who looks like you can hug her.

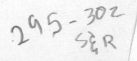

OTHER BOOKS YOU MAY ENJOY

free verse

free verse

Sarah Dooley

PUFFIN BOOKS

PUFFIN BOOKS
An imprint of Penguin Random House LLC
375 Hudson Street
New York, New York 10014

First published in the United States of America by G. P. Putnam's Sons,
an imprint of Penguin Random House LLC, 2016
Published by Puffin Books, an imprint of Penguin Random House LLC, 2017

THE LIBRARY OF CONGRESS HAS CATALOGED THE G. P. PUTNAM'S SONS EDITION AS FOLLOWS:

Dooley, Sarah.
Free verse / Sarah Dooley.
pages cm.
Summary: After her brother dies in a fire, Sasha Harless has no one left and nowhere to
turn, but soon discovers family she didn't know she had, and begins to heal through poetry.
ISBN 9780399165030 (hc)
[1. Families—Fiction. 2. Foster Home Care—Fiction. 3. Poetry—Fiction.
4. Grief—Fiction.]
I. Title.
PZ7.D72652 Fr 2016
[Fic]—dc23

Puffin Books ISBN 9780147509154

Printed in the United States of America

Bird images: EkaterinaP/Shutterstock. Paper images: Picsfive/Shutterstock

1 3 5 7 9 10 8 6 4 2

For Beth Anne
and all my library writers

part one

1

Nobody tells me this is the last time
I'll see my apartment off Route 10. Nobody but Michael
ever tells me anything, and Michael died. Still, I touch the
grooves on the counter where he used to dice potatoes
without a cutting board. I shuffle my sneakers against the
scuffs in the linoleum where he used to kick off his fireman boots, trading them for his grocery store shoes.

I want to say something. Something just right. But time
keeps moving and the words won't come, and my brother
isn't around to hear them anyway.

Phyllis, the foster mother the state of West Virginia has
picked for me, is still a stranger, despite the three days
I've spent pacing her unfamiliar house. She drapes an arm
across my shoulders, but it doesn't fit right, so she takes it
back. Before she leads me away, she checks the windows
to make sure they're locked. She mumbles something

about the thermostat but never manages to find it. She puts my jacket around my shoulders but doesn't make me use the sleeves. She leads me to the car.

"You didn't find your dress, Sasha?" she asks. Her question is pointless, since she left my key on the counter and locked the door. If I didn't find my dress abandoned in a closet or lost behind the landlord's couch, what difference does it make now? Strictly speaking, we weren't supposed to be in the apartment to begin with, but it was my only piece of clothing that looked okay for a funeral and my last excuse to be here.

I shake my head. I didn't actually look for the dress, not once I was inside. There were too many other things to look at and to think about.

Phyllis drives us back through town to her small house in one of the nicer neighborhoods in Caboose. She doesn't have a driveway, so she parks on the gravelly shoulder of Route 10. She cuts the engine and waits for me to move, then, when I don't, creaks her own door open. She loops around the front of the car and opens mine, too.

"We need to be back in the car in forty-five minutes."

The dress she puts me in is too loose in the chest and smells like grease and Avon, like somebody sprayed Skin So Soft on a plate of fried potatoes. She stands behind me, finger-combing my hair. It hasn't been washed in days. Nobody's played with my hair since my mother left, and it makes tears crawl up into the back of my throat. I swallow them down.

Phyllis's front door sticks, and she kicks it closed behind us with enough force to make it stick. She tugs the doorknob to be sure it locked. This is not one of those sweet small towns. People will steal your prescription medication. They will steal your copper wiring. They will steal your dog. The neighbor kids are out on the porch, bundled up against the cold. I've caught glimpses of them before, through the dead February trees that separate the two yards. The boy is digging a trench around the bottom step with a stick. The two little girls stop fighting over a toy truck long enough to stare us down with round green eyes. Phyllis ushers me into the car and closes the door. The girls go back to their truck. The older one wins and the younger one flings herself down in a tantrum. Even with the car door between us, I can hear her high wail cutting through the cold. I draw my feet up onto the seat, and when Phyllis slides behind the wheel, she reaches over and tugs my skirt down till it covers my knees.

"Hold on," she says. I don't think she's talking about the car ride.

The church smells more like perfume than air. Me and Michael would have stood in a corner and made fun of people's pantsuits and glittery brooches, but this is his funeral and all he does is lie still. I won't look at him. I stare instead at the flowers, which look as though they might be real, only I know they're not, because it's February and nothing much is blooming now. Through its burgundy carpet, the floor feels hollow, like I might fall through it if I step too hard.

The minister is only a minister on Sundays and when somebody dies or gets married. The rest of the time, he runs fire calls with Michael. He calls Michael his fallen brother, and I press fingernail prints into my palms. Michael wasn't anybody's brother except mine.

The pastor's eyes find me in the crowd, and I watch sadness deepen the lines on his face. I know all the faces and all the names of Michael's fellow firemen, but I can't always put them together. I check the program, which is printed slightly off center so that the last few lines of Psalm 23 curl around from the back. *Pastor: Allen Ramey*. Right.

Ramey talks about the man upstairs as though he's afraid to say the word *God* too loud. It's a simple service because both the man doing the talking and the man surrounded by flowers prefer things that way. Michael was never one for the dramatic, so Ramey keeps the service bare-bones short out of respect. *He was a good man. He sliced cuts of meat at the Save-Great by day and put out fires by night. He once literally saved a kitten from a tree, and got scratched so deep he had to get stitches.* A grim chuckle. *We hassled him for weeks over that one.*

4

Everything he says is true. Michael was a good man. He did work two jobs. He was the kind of guy who would go out of his way to save a kitten, even if he cussed it while he did. None of those things are the most important part of who he was, though. He was my brother. Michael was my brother, and now I don't have a brother.

"They don't make 'em like old Harless anymore," Ramey says. I wrap my arms around myself because there's nobody else to do it for me.

The cemetery is close to where Michael and I lived. Michael's firehouse only has one real fire truck, which is parked now at Michael's graveside, a flag hanging from its raised ladder. The rest of the fleet is made up of people's old Chevy S-10s, with red lights Krazy-Glued onto the dashboards. The squad is small and mostly volunteer. I only know their last names, because Michael called them by *Ramey* or *Kamm* or *Sweeney*, usually with jokes or swearing after. Most of them are young, and most hold other jobs, like Michael. I see them around town, salting fries at Burger Bargain, shelving old TVs at the pawnshop, dodging potholes with school buses.

I think maybe Ramey's going to start talking again, but he just stares at the ground and waits. A radio crackles and Michael's name is called, as if he's being asked to respond to a fire.

"Harless, this is dispatch, please respond."

We wait for his voice to come over the air.

"Harless, this is dispatch, come back?"

Come back! I think.

"Dispatch to Harless, please respond."

He doesn't, and he doesn't, and he *doesn't*.

"Dispatch to Harless," the voice on the radio says. "You are relieved of your duty. God bless you for your service."

Somebody sobs. I think maybe it's Phyllis. She never met Michael, so she probably doesn't know he'd be embarrassed by all the fuss. He always said he wanted to be cremated and then scattered on the grounds of the fire, if that's what took him. Which is stupid, so I never told anybody.

The prayers and flags and radio static are all too much to take in. I expected the dirt and the hole in the ground, but I didn't know the hole would have neat corners and this metal structure, now lowering the box out of sight with a low hum. It reminds me of the air conditioner in our apartment, which is a silly thing to think about.

Michael's gone into the hole before I can stop him. I'm supposed to throw in a handful of earth, but instead I hold the two fistfuls of black dirt. I'm pretty sure I got half an earthworm. I smell the dirt. I taste it, and it tastes like rare meat or lost teeth. My lip and chin are smeared with grime. Polite mourners turn their faces away. Phyllis takes a wet wipe from her purse and cleans my chin as casually as she would her glasses.

2

There's a rectangle of weak, late February sunlight on the floor of Phyllis's kitchen. It used to be over by the ice-cream churn, but as evening comes on, it inches toward the bag of red potatoes propped up beside the fridge. I haven't moved in a while.

Phyllis is humming her way around the kitchen, adjusting things that don't look like they need it. There aren't any dirty dishes in the sink, but every so often she plucks something out of the drainer, looks at it closely, and then whips it over to the sink to rewash. Twice, she's heated water in the kettle and forgotten to make tea. Neither of us has said anything in a while, except for when her humming gives way to a word or two: "... *green and shady* ..." "... *river's in flood* ..." This is how we've spent the last week, nervous and quiet, together in the kitchen.

As foster mothers go, Phyllis could probably be worse.

Of course, she's the only foster mother I've ever had, so I don't have much to compare her to. She's kind, and she cooks. She's sweet to her animals, a nosy cat and a sagging dog, both of whom live outside. She's thoughtful enough that she's taken some time off work, even though her boss has called twice to see when she's coming back. I don't know her very well yet, and maybe we're not talking much, but I'm relieved I don't have to be here by myself. I can't think of anything lonelier than a stranger's kitchen with nobody in it.

"You hungry yet?" she asks me, checking the oven clock, which is still set to daylight savings instead of standard time because she doesn't know how to reprogram it. You have to subtract an hour when you look at it. It'll be right again in a couple of weeks.

It's impossible to think about food, let alone eat any. I shake my head.

She starts cooking anyway, dirtying up some of the dishes from the drainer.

"Help me, would you, Sasha?" she asks after a while. Each thing that happens with Phyllis—I can't help but compare it to the way things were before. Michael didn't let me cook. Maybe because he was a firefighter and he didn't want me to use the stove. I don't know how to do much, and anyway, the smell of potatoes browning in butter is making my stomach feel swimmy. I back away, shaking my head.

"You don't have to eat it," Phyllis says, tipping a mess of steaming potatoes onto a plate. She runs cold water in the frying pan and steam hisses up out of the sink. "But I could use a little help with the dishes." Her words are mild, and her tone is kind. "Sometimes it helps a person to keep busy."

At home, I'd have been busy with studying or putting on music to clean house with Michael. Every so often, when the mess got too huge, we'd put on one of our favorite albums—something old, like Bob Dylan or Elvis— and we would whip around the apartment armed with a broom or a vacuum or a bottle of Windex, and by evening we would be worn out from laughing and the place would look arguably worse than it did before, and we would go to sleep happy. I can't remember ever washing a dish that was already clean, or cooking something that didn't come from a box in the freezer.

We eat in the living room, in front of the TV, only neither of us turns it on. I manage a bite or two of potatoes, but there are too many onions and not enough ketchup and my stomach still hurts. After dinner, Phyllis brings out the acoustic guitar with its bumper stickers and scratches, lifting it from a case lined with nicked red velveteen. I have never heard anybody play the guitar the way she does, a string at a time, not chords. She doesn't look at written music. When she plays, she closes her eyes. There is no makeup on her cheeks, and her hair must be its natural color, because I have never seen this shade of gold-coming-on-silver on a box. She's not a large person, but when she plays the guitar, her shoulders draw up taller and her legs relax out longer and her neck—I swear, her neck grows three inches as she tosses her head back and breathes songs up to the sky.

I watch her fingers most: nails even but unpolished, fingers calloused and stubby. I like the way the skin dents in when she presses a guitar string. Her fingers are strong like Michael's. Michael's hands saved people from fires. Phyllis's hands make music to distract the people left behind. She does not demand that I listen, but I'm caught, sitting on the floor next to the door, watching her fingers. There is a rug half under me, thin with years, on top of plywood. The way the strings snap back into place when she lets them go washes me in sadness. Like nothing you do ever really makes a difference.

My mother used to sing, just like Phyllis. She had a song about sunshine she liked to sing in cold weather, and I swear I still get warmer whenever I hear it. She sang songs to make the rain go away and songs to get us out of bed in the morning. I used to love hearing her voice.

There was one song, though, that I never liked to hear. She used to sing it on her saddest days. It's all about a caged bird trying to get free. Phyllis does not look up or act startled when I start to sing along. I remember the words. I remember them in my mother's voice, and that's what comes out of me, high and sad and longing.

There's this thing that happens sometimes.

The first time, I was eight. A few days after Michael and I got left alone, we were carrying groceries in from the car and I dropped the eggs. He'd told me six or eight times already to be careful, but I was certain I could handle them. This was the first normal thing we'd done since burying our father, and neither one of us was in very good shape. Michael had already snapped at one of his coworkers at the Save-Great for putting the granola bars on top of the bread, and now I'd gone and ruined the eggs. I hoped for just a second that they had survived; that the Styrofoam container had somehow protected them. But then I saw yolk oozing out.

I looked up and saw Michael's face, angry and tired and so much older than it had been the week before.

And then I looked up and I saw Michael's face again, now devastated and frightened, almost the way it looked at our father's funeral. I thought it odd that his expression changed so quickly. And then I looked down because my knuckles hurt, and I found out that I wasn't holding any of the grocery bags anymore, and the Styrofoam egg container was smashed into pieces, and the passenger-side mirror was hanging sideways off my dad's truck, and I was out of breath.

Michael took three full, shaky breaths, so slow and so

loud I could hear them over the start of my own hiccupping sobs, and then he simply opened his arms and I flung myself into them and we both held on so tightly.

It happened a second time last year, when Chris McKenzie died.

I was in math class when Mr. Powell, the guidance counselor, stepped into the room. He had this look on his face that made my stomach feel cold, because I'd seen that look on my brother's face twice and it never led anywhere good.

I didn't know Chris McKenzie well. He was an eighth grader and I was only in sixth. I knew where he'd been yesterday evening, though. I'd seen him setting things on fire in the parking lot of the Save-Great, watching bits of paper bag whoosh upward in flames, raining sparks down to where he stood. My brother was a firefighter, and even if he wasn't, I'd have known it was stupid to light things on fire, but I was a sixth grader and Chris was in eighth. All I did was give him a mean look.

Still, there was a little part of me that understood. Sometimes you do something crazy because you can't stand to not do anything. That was Chris McKenzie, lighting fires because he needed his hands and his mind to be full. Bright sparks, dangerous things. They command attention. They distract. I didn't know what it was Chris needed to be distracted from, but I recognized the need itself.

And then sometimes you do something crazy because

there's nothing left to distract you. When Mr. Powell speaks, when he tells you what has happened to Chris— or, rather, what Chris has done to himself—there's so much fear and so much sadness welling up inside you that you can't hold it all. Yesterday Chris was a person lighting things on fire at the SaveGreat, and today there is no such person, and you might have been the last person to see him when he was still real. Your brain goes from overload to total shutdown, and then you blink, or at least you think that's what you did, only you find out you're not in class anymore. You're standing behind your school, next to the Dumpsters, where the kitchen staff sneaks out to smoke, and your knuckles are scraped but you don't know why. And Anthony Tucker is standing three feet behind you, breathing heavily and looking terrified, with his hands up, like you're some wild thing that might charge him.

"Sasha?" He's the school bully. Since you were second graders, he has followed you around, tugging at your braid, stepping on the backs of your shoes, and putting gum in your hair. You've never heard his voice sound anything except taunting, but now it's dead serious and scared and he sounds about six years old. "Hey. What did that Dumpster ever do to you?"

And you run past him because you can't face the fact that the worst bully in the whole school just saw you lose your head for a minute.

I'm not crazy. I'm not. It's just that there are days when

the scared and the mad and the sad inside me get so big that my body can't hold them. And then they come out, and maybe I'm a little bit scared that it *does* make me crazy, but I'd never say so.

When Phyllis is done singing about caged birds, I open my eyes. There is a weird sound, like a hard strum of a guitar. I am on my feet and Phyllis is half up from her chair, fingertips stretching out in the air like she's trying to catch raindrops or the seconds that just went by. The guitar is on the floor with its strings pointing every which way, splinters of wood poking out along the side.

I work on catching my breath. In-in-in quick. Out long. In-in-in quick. Out long.

Phyllis, without her guitar, looks small. Her hands seem fragile.

"Well. I guess I played the wrong song," she says. There is nothing musical about her voice now. She sinks into her chair and goes still.

3

Michael leapt sideways and managed to catch the Frisbee even though I wasn't very good at throwing it. We'd been playing for half an hour, and he had yet to miss a catch. My third-grade teacher, who just yesterday finished wrangling us through a Memorial Day craft, would have said we were being disrespectful, playing Frisbee in a cemetery with fallen soldiers and stuff, and I told Michael as much, but he said if he were buried here, he wouldn't mind two kids having fun on his lawn.

"Any soldier grew up here would know there's no other place to play that's sort of flat and doesn't have trees," he said.

Michael had been planning to join the military; had been impossible to live with for weeks because of all the working out and eating healthy and all the hooyah-ing. Then the mine fell down on our dad and everything stopped. Now certain things were starting again—I was going to school, Michael was back at work—but there was no more working out and no more talk of going anywhere and Michael hardly ever smiled. We played a lot of Frisbee. We hiked, too, and ran sprints, and we were building a fence between our building and the house next door, but it was only half finished, because we ran out of wood and energy.

Michael hated Caboose. Always had. Some of my earliest memories were of Michael telling me stories about Someplace Else. He told me all about how in real places, there were trains that ran under the city and that they could take you anywhere you wanted to go, and nobody had to drive an old pickup truck that broke down every two days. How in some places you could live in a house up on stilts so the ocean could drift in and out underneath. He told me about planes that landed on water, and about night skylines that made the stars look faded. There were a lot of places Michael wanted to go, but they all sounded awfully far away.

Even now that he'd stopped talking about leaving, he couldn't help but mutter under his breath about how much he hated Caboose: "Only place I know where kids can have a game of Frisbee and a dang séance in the same five minutes." I wasn't sure what a séance was or why he sounded so bent out of shape about it. He threw the Frisbee so hard, I heard it whistle past my ear. I ran to catch it. I'd missed it about thirty times already, but Michael hadn't given up on me yet.

"Watch out!"

His warning came a second too late. My shin connected with a gravestone, and the Frisbee and I were suddenly side by side, airborne. I snatched the bit of plastic out of the last six inches of air before it would have smacked into the grass. It never touched a blade, only the grass stains on my fingers. I lay still, catching my breath.

Michael's footsteps pounded up behind me. "You all right? Hey . . ." He dropped to his knees next to me. He looked mad, but not at me. He'd been mad a lot lately, ever since our dad. He got sad a lot, too, but I don't think he knew I could tell. "Hey, sorry," he said, helping me up to sitting. "I'm sorry, sis, I didn't mean to throw it so hard."

I was pretty sure I could taste mud in my mouth, and I couldn't get my breath to go back out all the way. I sat for a minute, gasping, before my air all came out in a whoosh. Michael ran a shaky hand down his face, leaving a trail of mud to match my own.

"You all right?" he asked again.

"I got it," I said, holding up the Frisbee, and his eyes moved from my face to the toy and back again. I waited to see what he would do next. Ever since he got to be my only family, I could never tell how he would act about things.

A grin spread across his muddy face, and I could feel my own grin come out.

"Well, you play Frisbee like you doggone mean it, Sasha," he said with pride in his voice.

• • •

For some reason, after I smash the guitar, I can't stop thinking about that Frisbee. Can't stop thinking about Michael's pride when I finally caught it. He gave up everything for me: his dreams of the military, of college, of subways and ocean views and living someplace better than here. At eighteen, he took over being my parent and he never once complained. He wanted me to catch the doggone Frisbee, and even back then, I think I'd have flown if it meant doing what he asked me to.

And Michael asked me to do a lot of things over the years. Ace my spelling test. Read a chapter a night. *Brush your doggone teeth before they fall out of your head!* But there was one thing he asked for more than any other, and he spent the last few years of his life getting me ready for it.

So I'm a little glad he doesn't know that when I finally do leave Caboose, I don't even manage to wear shoes.

I can't stay in the house with Phyllis. She's sitting in a chair, not moving. Her hands are empty. Her hands are empty and it's my fault. She's not going to want me. I don't even know her, and I've gone and wrecked her life. I'm all the way down past Town Center before I realize I'm still in my socks. I've wrecked those, too. I'm good at wrecking things.

Route 10 is the main road through town and the only one with a yellow line. Once I cross the Gillums Bridge, I feel more at home. There isn't enough of Caboose to have very many parts of town, but there is, at least, a poor side and a rich side. Phyllis lives on the rich side, where the houses are set down single-lane paved streets. The grass is cut even in summer, and it more or less survives the winter. In spring, people will plant flowers in the boxes and pots that now stand empty by the walk. Even on the rich side, folks are mostly poor. They've just had a splash or two of better luck.

On my side of town, houses cluster along the highway or curl through the floodplain on dirt roads over and again washed out. Weed-strangled vacant lots lurk in between mushed-down brown yards, which, come summer, will still be more dirt than grass. Instead of flower boxes, yards here are dotted with bikes and rusting lawn mowers, dogs chained to plastic igloo-shaped shelters, and sets of tires marked with FOR SALE signs. It's February, and the weeds gripping the vacant houses have been beaten down by rain and a couple of good snows. The sagging houses lean low against their neighbors, an occasional filthy patch of ice refusing to melt in the shadow. Here and there, a pretty house pops up—trim repainted, fence in good repair—and dogs patrol those houses with a suspicious eye toward a lone girl walking.

Dust collects on the insides of windows in what used to be my family's favorite breakfast spot. I can still make out the *w* and *y* of *Railway* and the *Din* of *Diner*, but it's been years since the low-slung building's smelled like eggs and bacon, or anything besides high water. Caboose hasn't had a bad flood in years, but with the creek lapping at our yards every time it rains, everything on this side of town smells like mold and mud.

I walk past three empty buildings and a Goodwill. Two more empties and a home décor shop called Dolly's Primitives, which I predict will last all of two months. Sometimes people open businesses and try to make the downtown thrive, but nothing ever stays long. At the end of the block, I walk past the narrow building that used to be Get Reel Video Rental, before it was Sugar Shaker Nightclub, before it was Honey Ham Cafe. Now it's Cupcake Emporium, only it isn't Cupcake Emporium anymore, because the windows that used to say so are busted out. I see glass twinkling on the sidewalk. I see yellow fire tape. I see signs that say DANGER. I look away.

On the other side of the street, birds are sorting through an overgrown lot for seed. A boy, maybe seven, throws a rock. They all fly, the birds and the boy, back to where they came from.

A human being in good shape, on good roads, can walk about twenty miles in a day. I looked it up online once, back when me and Michael used to stay up late talking about all the ways we could leave. He told me that was crazy—we weren't going to walk out. We were going to plan and study and take our time and get me a scholarship to some awesome college somewhere. But all his talk about getting trapped made my clothes feel too tight and my breath come short. I needed to know there was a quick way out, should I ever notice that I was getting comfortable with the idea of staying here forever. Michael made it sound like I might someday wake up and realize I was forty and that I'd never been anywhere and could never escape.

By late evening, I've learned that a human girl in okay shape, in thickets, carrying her belongings, can walk about three miles.

Then she panics and hides in a culvert and loses track of time for a while.

Then she goes to sleep.

When I wake up, it's thunderstorming, and I stay in the culvert, which fills more and more with water. I cannot make myself stand. My joints stay folded. My limbs stay useless. The water rises.

The things in the suitcase I've brought with me are soaked. I keep the clothes. They'll dry. I leave the soggy picture of me and my brother. You can't see our faces anymore.

All the way down East Avenue, I look back and I see

that little white speck of ruined photo paper. When it's finally out of sight, I run back. I pick it up.

Michael would tell me what the clouds mean. How long the storm will last. I take shelter in the doorway of the Baptist church at dusk. They can't kick you out of the doorway of a church.

After they kick me out of the doorway of the church, assuming, I suppose, that I'm a teen of the rock-throwing variety—the church has lost three stained-glass windows this year alone, and is adorned now with less spiritual plywood—I cross the train tracks, slippery socks on rusty ties. I find a railroad spike, pick it up, throw it as hard as I can. Thunder crashes right when I should have heard a clatter. I needed the clatter, the noise. That's why I threw the spike in the first place.

I stand still for a while because I don't know what else to do. Then I hear the ruckus of train wheels approaching, and I hunker down on the thin strip between the train tracks and the creek. I press my hands over my ears. The train roars by, roars away. The creek roars by, keeps roaring by.

When the rain lets up, I walk some more. I stop to pick up fistfuls of mud. I kick rocks and beer cans into the creek. I fight through thickets. I untangle brambles. After I've fallen no less than three times in the dirt, I stop for a minute. I braid my hair.

· · ·

Night happens. The kind with stars. Then morning does. The kind with birds.

When the wind goes out of my sails and I admit defeat, I loop back the way I came. I pass everything again, going in the other direction, but it's all so gray and familiar that I have to work to see each building as a separate place. I pass closed stores and empty houses. I pass a fire station with one truck and one less fireman than it used to have. I pass a pawnshop full of wedding rings. I pass skinny men on front porches looking at me with suspicion in their eyes. Michael always warned me away from this part of town, told me the druggies weren't safe to be around. He wouldn't like me walking here alone. I want to walk faster, but I only seem to have one speed. I trudge on through the worst part of my little town.

I sit on the bench at Town Center, the little park marked with a rusting red train caboose. I gaze at the park's sign, which is missing a C: TOWN   ENTER. I don't feel cold or tired anymore, but I can't imagine ever doing anything again besides sitting on this bench. I wait for night to fall. I wait for somebody to find me.

4

Phyllis comes to see me at the hospital in the northern part of the county. Her empty hands hang like wilted flowers.

They make me stay at the hospital for hours because I walked without shoes for so long that I hurt my feet and because I didn't drink anything for the two days I went walking. They poke me with a needle to give me water. They smile with toothpaste mouths and they undo my braids and wash my hair.

"I wish you'd told me you was going, Sasha," Phyllis says. "I would have packed you some sandwiches, at least."

I can't turn over without tugging the needle out of my arm. I lie perfectly still.

"Egg salad," Phyllis says. "You like egg salad?"

···

A couple days later, me and Phyllis sit on her porch in folding chairs, eating egg salad sandwiches. We're both bundled up against the cold of early March. It's four a.m. This is when I finally got hungry.

The neighbor comes out on his porch, cursing, and a child's shoe skitters out with him. He nearly falls. After he kicks the shoe back in the house, he locks the door.

The neighbor is dressed in blue coveralls with reflective stripes down the sides. That means he's on his way to the coal mines. He might have worked with my dad, with Ben. I picture Ben raising one coal-darkened hand to this neighbor as they arrive on the job. I raise my hand, like I did the day Ben left.

The neighbor waves back with a grimy hand that I know will never come clean, like he has a tattoo of coal dirt. Phyllis and I watch him climb into the blue pickup truck and disappear down Route 10. She says, "That's Hubert Harless. Any relation?"

I shrug and sigh. There are a passel of Harlesses in Caboose. I'm probably not related to all of them, but nobody claimed me after Michael. I hope I'm not related to somebody named Hubert. That's one of those names you see on national TV when someone from West Virginia gets interviewed. I don't want people in other states to think we're all named things like Hubert and Bucky and Junior. We have Williams. We have Gavins and Garretts and Sams. We have one less Michael than we did before, but still, we have Michaels. I can't deny, though, that there are people around here with names and nicknames like Hubert and Bucky and Junior. I may or may not be related to one.

Phyllis has a cat that won't leave me alone. She bumps her body against my lower legs. She stands up and puts her feet on my knees. She smells my sandwich.

"You tell Stella to get down," Phyllis says. "She don't need your sandwich."

I've already picked apart the last corner of my sandwich. I drop the rest on the porch. "She can have it."

A couple days later, Phyllis and I sit on the front porch, eating egg salad sandwiches. It's four a.m. This is the next time I got hungry.

It's ten a.m. and I'm still on the porch. The porch is better than the house. More to see and less to think about. Hubert Harless waves his hand to me now without me having to raise mine first. His two little daughters follow him across the porch. It's a Saturday. It's unseasonably warm for March. He's got overalls on today instead of coveralls, so he must not be going to work. The two little girls wear diapers and long T-shirts.

Hubert Harless has a wife named Shirley who stays in the house. If I look out Phyllis's kitchen window, I can see Shirley at the sink, washing cake pans.

Hubert Harless's son is named Mikey. I'm surprised there's been another Michael Harless in the town of Caboose this whole time and I never knew it. But it's not as hard as you'd think to not know people in Caboose. People keep to themselves. You can end up knowing the lady at the Save-Great cash register better than you know your own family, if they don't live next door.

According to Phyllis, Mikey Harless doesn't belong to Shirley. He only belongs to Hubert. He's nine years old. He has glasses.

It eats at me all weekend. I have to know. So late Sunday morning, I knock on the door and ask Shirley if we're related.

"You're Benjermin's girl, ain't you?" she asks. She isn't mispronouncing my father's name. It was his mother who misspelled it.

I wait for her to answer my question.

"Benjermin's daddy and Hubert's daddy was brothers," Shirley says.

"That makes Hubert my cousin."

"Benjermin's daddy and Hubert's daddy didn't talk to each other for twenty years."

I mull. "I think that still makes Hubert my cousin."

She goes back to her cake pans. Because she doesn't lock the door, I follow her in.

Shirley's kitchen is decorated in apple everything: curtains, window trim, cutting board. There are plastic apples in a bowl—at least, I think they're plastic. The kitchen is nicer than the rest of the house, like Shirley spends a lot of time here. There is a newish computer whirring on a desk in the corner.

Shirley puts biscuits on the table, in reach of me. They're covered by a dish towel with apples on it. Mikey Harless sits in a corner of the kitchen, on the floor. He colors with a black crayon. He doesn't look up when I come in.

"Mikey, run and get your daddy and the girls," Shirley says. "Lunch is up." Her voice is high-pitched and cheerful.

Mikey doesn't move. I see his eyes flick toward her and away. He colors through the face of the little kid in his coloring book. The face disappears under black crayon so thick you could scratch designs in it with your fingernail.

Shirley looks like she's ready to speak again, maybe not so cheerful this time, when my cousin Hubert comes in, carrying one daughter and leading one by the hand. The baby in his arms has elbow dimples and knee dimples and cheek dimples, and her belly sticks out, round, over the top of her diaper. She keeps grabbing Hubert by the beard and tugging on his ears and poking him in the eyes. She says syllables that aren't quite words yet, but she clearly has some strong opinions. The little girl he's leading by the hand is all angles, long lines of bone with knobs of elbow and knee. She keeps sniffling and hiking her diaper up with her free hand.

I wonder whether these little girls are my cousins, too. I guess Mikey is, and I suppose Shirley is my cousin by marriage. Is there such a thing as a cousin by marriage?

The Harlesses over on East Avenue might be my cousins, too; nobody's ever told me different. And maybe I'm related to the Harlesses on North Road. Or even the Harlesses that live a couple miles down the highway leading out. It's too small a town for there to be many unrelated people with the same last name.

But these Harlesses live on Route 10, next to Phyllis. I'm fascinated. I eat a biscuit.

Hubert Harless tells me he never met my father till they were working together in the Hardwater coal mine.

"I heard tell about Ben," Hubert says, scratching his beard, which is as wiry as a scrub brush. "I heard stories. Didn't sound like a bad fella. I didn't have nothing against your daddy. It's just, our families didn't talk. Dad and Uncle Arlie had a fallen-out." He means "falling-out," but I like the soft sound of the way he says it.

"How come?" I talk with my mouth full of biscuit.

"Don't know," Hubert says. He talks with his mouth full of biscuit, too.

"Well, what stories did you hear?"

Hubert smiles slow under his mustache. "Ben was a lot like your brother, Michael. Had all these big plans, never carried through on a one of 'em."

"You knew Michael?" Somewhere inside, I shake. Hearing Michael's name still takes away all the oxygen from the room for a second.

"Lot of folks did. Good man, your brother."

I put my biscuit back on my plate. I think I'm finished.

"'Course, Ben had that stubborn streak a lot of us old-timers have." Hubert's smile grows wide enough to peek out from the corners of his mustache. "Hard to miss him trying to catch Judy's eye."

I act casual, even though my heartbeat speeds up at the sound of my mother's name. "What do you mean?"

"Your old man chased that poor girl around Caboose for upwards of a year before she broke down and agreed to go out with him."

There is a sensation deep in my chest that feels like the ache you get in your teeth when you drink something cold. A term I have never completely understood—*heartache*—suddenly feels literal. Something right where my heart lives is hurting. I get this picture in my head of my mother, who I only remember in pieces—hands, hair, earrings, lipstick, and a sad line or two from her favorite song—being chased by my father, who I remember so vividly I can still smell his aftershave. The biscuit I've already eaten starts turning somersaults in my stomach. I don't remember my father as a man who should have had to chase after anybody, least of all somebody who didn't turn out to want him.

"You know how he proposed marriage, don't you?"

I don't. But I don't like admitting it, so I pick a crumb off the biscuit and eat it so I've got my mouth full and don't have to answer.

"Man climbed a telephone pole. Started hollering down, asking your mama to marry him. He sat at the top of that pole more'n two hours, till somebody was able to round her up. He was drunker'n a skunk, of course. Least he was when he went up. By the time she finally said yes—probably just to get him down off that dang utility pole—he'd more or less sobered up. Had the ring with him the whole time."

Mikey snickers.

"That doesn't sound true," I say.

Hubert's eyes twinkle. "Well, that's the story, anyway. They say the cops were waiting, gonna haul him off to jail, but they turned a blind eye because a man does what he's got to do to get a woman to marry him. Ain't that right, babe?" Hubert glances over his shoulder at Shirley, who hasn't joined us at the table. She's wiping down the cutting board, which already looks clean.

"What?" Shirley glances up, looking genuinely startled.

Hubert lets out the smallest of sighs, almost quick enough to miss. "Never mind. Got any more biscuits?"

• • •

Phyllis tucks me in, even though I'm too old to be tucked in. I tell her about my cousins next door, and her forehead gathers into deeper wrinkles. Wisps of her graying hair are forever escaping her messy ponytail, and she's always sucking one of her cheeks in like she's chewing on the inside of it and thinking.

"I don't know if I like you wandering around," is all she says.

I want to ask whether Phyllis has any kids of her own. They'd have to be grown now; she's an older lady. I'm careful not to point that out when I ask, "Do you have kids?"

"Two sons," she says. "Sam and Miles."

"Where are they now?"

"Sam teaches welding at a trade school in Indiana. He married a sweet little girl he met when he was in trade school himself."

"How'd he end up in Indiana?" With Michael's years of talking in my ear about getting out of Caboose, I can't help but be fascinated by the ways that people leave. I'll bet Sam at least managed to wear shoes when he took off.

"That's where Mary's people are from."

"Did Miles move away, too?"

Phyllis smooths the quilt on both sides of me and turns

off the lamp, so that only the light from the hall bathroom spills into the little bedroom. In the dim light, Phyllis looks older, or sadder. Lines trace down from the corners of her eyes like tear tracks that stuck. She stands abruptly, makes it all the way to the door before she turns.

"Miles is with your brother. Good night, Sasha." She goes before I can ask any more questions.

5

I figure out how to get the back door open. There is prying involved, which explains the hammer propped next to it. The back door leads to a tiny yard, where Chip, Phyllis's droopy dog, woofs a soft hello. He doesn't bother to pick his head up off the cold ground.

It's two forty-five a.m. I figure I've got an hour before Phyllis comes looking for me. Two forty-five a.m. in early March in Caboose is peaceful, but not quiet. I hear a dog barking a few yards over, but Chip pays no attention. A train's wheels rattle, not on the nearest tracks but on the branch that cuts off toward Vineland. From the highway, I can hear trucks. Most people hate the emergency brakes they call "Jake brakes" because of how loud they are, but I like how you can hear them from a distance. They sound like the road, and the road sounds like keeping a promise I made to Michael.

For the moment, I make do with exploring my new yard, and the one beside it. There aren't a lot of good fences in Caboose. There are tall ones keeping people out of the abandoned mine sites past city limits. There is a picket one between the grocery store and the trailer park behind it. A few of the nicer houses in town have privacy fencing around their yards, usually chain link with green or white plastic woven through for privacy, but sometimes something fancier, like stone.

Phyllis doesn't have a fence. Not even a hedge. It's easy to wander into my cousin's backyard.

The house has asbestos siding, which you aren't supposed to use, but it's fireproof. The window glass is wavy, the way it looks when it's older than your parents. I have to stand on my tiptoes to see in the nearest window, and on the other side of the glass, there is a quilt tacked up, pink and ratty. I can't see anything else, but I hear a faint snore.

There isn't a back door in the Harless house, but there's a storm door lying in the weeds. I wonder whether it came off the front door or if somebody put it here so they could build a back door later. There are tripping hazards in the tall grass of the yard as well: a hole with a shovel sticking out of it, somebody's old work boot, a pile of broken bricks. The next window I come to, the glass is newer, not wavy with age. It has a sticker on it with the silhouette of a fireman carrying a baby. I know from elementary school and from Michael that these stickers are used to let a fire-fighter know there are children in this room who need saving. As firefighter deaths go, I think rescuing a baby would have been a better way for Michael. I've never seen a sticker of a fireman carrying a cupcake.

There is no quilt on the other side of this glass. It takes a minute of staring before I can work out what I'm look-ing at. Then my heart thumps with surprise. I am rattled.

Mikey Harless stares out of the window, his nose inches from my own. He doesn't budge, and I don't, either. He's wearing his glasses. He's still in his jeans, like he never went to bed.

We stand and stare at each other.

When Mikey retreats into the darkness of his room, all at once, as though remembering something he'd forgotten, I head back into Chip's yard and sneak through the dark-ened house. I don't want Phyllis to know I was in a stare-down with Mikey Harless for almost half an hour. She has not exactly *forbidden* me to sneak out after dark, and I'd like to keep it that way.

We eat egg salad on the porch. I think Phyllis probably doesn't have egg salad for every breakfast when I'm not here. I think about the days before I came, wonder how much time she spent on this porch, watching the sunrise. How much time she'll spend here when I've gone wher-ever it is foster kids go when a foster mom gets tired of them. We pet Stella and watch streaks of pink work their way up from the tips of the trees. We wave good-bye to Hubert Harless and watch his truck disappear down Main Street.

On Monday, Grace, the social worker from the county, comes. I met her right after Michael, but I don't remember a whole lot about those days. Today, I really look at her. She doesn't dress the way I would have thought, like in a business suit or something. She wears khaki pants that aren't very dressy, more like cargos with a ton of pockets. She wears a polo shirt with a logo on it that doesn't seem to be from her job. I like her kind eyes, but not the pressed-in corners of her lips.

She says I have to go to school. I missed a week after Michael, and then the school went on spring break and I was spared from it another week, but now it's time to get back into a routine.

I do *not* think about school.

I *do* think about what Phyllis will do while I'm gone. She doesn't have a guitar to keep her busy. I can't always stand to think about what happened to it, but I know she doesn't have one and I know it's my fault. She tells me she's going back to work, since I'm going back to school. She works above the Laundromat, where Mr. Cardman has his lawyer's office. She types things.

The elementary school bus comes in the darkness of

Thursday morning. Mikey climbs on it and it carries him away. His sister Marla screams from the porch. She wants to go on the school bus, too. I want to offer her my spot.

My bus, which goes to the middle and high schools out of town, comes twenty minutes later. I have to walk down the street and around the corner to the sagging red bus house to catch it. The driver wears a uniform and doesn't smile. The kids mostly wear jeans and sneakers, a few skirts here and there. The whole bus smells like sulfur water and cigarette smoke. I tried on almost everything I own last night to find the perfect back-to-school outfit, but I maybe don't own one of those. I tug my jeans up and my T-shirt down.

There are no empty seats. I'm paralyzed. The driver tells me twice to find a seat.

I choose a strange face to sit next to. I'm not friends with anybody on the bus, but I know most of the faces. This girl, I don't know. She's a small-looking girl and doesn't seem likely to hurt me. I sit beside her and she scoots toward the window. Her long brown hair swings forward so I can't see her face. I fix my eyes on my knees, but out of the corner of my eye, I can't help but see her farm-muddy jeans and worn cowboy boots. Her clothes make me relax a little. She doesn't appear stuck-up or scary.

School is a thirty-minute bus ride out of Caboose and over the mountain. I watch mailboxes flash past as we start our climb. Three of them say Harless. I see the entrance to the Hardwater mine, long closed and abandoned. Heavy chains hold hands across the weed-strangled road leading in. This is the last place Ben ever drove his truck, five years ago now. I remember him driving away that evening. The fading sound of his ancient country music—Dwight Yoakam that morning—floated back to me and Michael, the two of us standing in the driveway in a sweet summer night full of lightning bugs and the smell of cut grass.

The news came late the next morning. The actual news, I mean: cameras and microphones, and reporters wanting to know not only what happened up at Hardwater—a cave-in, miners trapped and unaccounted for—but how it was affecting our small community. For days, bedsheets hung on porch rails and tree limbs, painted with messages like "God be with our miners" and "Prayers for Joe and the others" and "Keep the faith." I remember reporters on CNN talking about how they were being well fed and housed by the families of the miners while they covered the stories. Michael, who was fresh out of high school and trying to get fit enough to pass the tests for the Navy, stopped training and drove out to the mine instead, helping with the search and rescue efforts like a lot of younger guys in Caboose. I rode out with him a few times, and sat in the cab of the truck, which one of the accounted-for miners had brought home to us. I scraped patterns into old cigarette grime on the dashboard. I watched Michael as he stood outside the cab, finishing a cigarette of his own. Watched the lights on the fire trucks flash in his eyes.

It took the town of Caboose five days to find our people. By then, we already knew. When it was confirmed, the town held five funerals, including Ben's. They were televised, both locally and on CNN, and afterward, people drifted back into their homes and locked the doors. Still, nobody wanted to take down the bedsheets, and a lot of them hung until the paint washed off and the paisley print faded. By then, most of the sheets were nothing more than rags, impossibly knotted around tree limbs.

I shake off the memory as the bus pulls into Engine Creek, where the high school kids go. Next stop, on down to Bent Tree, is the middle school, which smells like waffles and glue guns. We are herded into the cafeteria, where we sit until the first bell rings at five of eight. I'm expecting to start in homeroom, but instead, Mr. Powell steps from his office into my path as I go by.

"Do you have a minute, Sasha?"

As if you can say no to the school guidance counselor. I've seen Mr. Powell ever since the day I ended up beside the Dumpster. At first, he just wanted to make sure I wasn't going to run out of the school again. Nobody expected the visits with Mr. Powell to go on as long as they have, but apparently I truly do have some type of "issue." The trouble is, nobody's ever told me what. I know I get nervous and think of all the bad things that might happen, and that sometimes it gets so overwhelming that I have to hide out in the girls' bathroom until my stomach stops hurting. I have a class period that I go to in the morning that's supposed to help me manage what my paperwork calls an "emotional disorder." Michael always said it was a load of crap; that any kid whose mom had up and left town when she was five and whose dad got killed in the mines when she was eight was bound to have some "friggin' issues." But he never asked the school to stop sending me to Mr. Powell, which, deep down, always worried me a little, like maybe Michael thought my "friggin' issues" were more serious than he let on.

He's kind of pointless, Mr. Powell, and so are his sessions, but I don't mind him much. Sometimes he can get me out of tests or help me with my homework. Seventh-grade algebra is no picnic, so I don't mind telling my teacher I need to go see the counselor that period.

Seeing Mr. Powell is not a good idea after all. The books on his shelf are always in the same order, so I know he doesn't read them. I can't blame him. They have titles like *Depression in Adolescents* and *Our Youth, Our Future*.

I have a hard time paying attention to the right things in Mr. Powell's room. I notice that his clock battery has died and we're stuck at ten after five. I notice that he's worked his way down through the yellow layer on his Post-it cube and now he's working on the pink layer.

I don't remember what he says.

I walk into my first class late, clutching a bright pink Post-it that says not to count me tardy. I don't want to get in trouble, so I don't say anything or look at anybody. After a while, it's like I'm not here.

In between classes, I sneak into the girls' bathroom. I carry my brown paper lunch sack, which Phyllis filled with egg salad sandwiches. I hide in one of the stalls, on the toilet. I feel scared for no reason. It's strange, being back. Everything here is so normal, like no time has passed. Everything's been different in the two weeks since Michael died, and now I'm back at school, with rows of eraser-pink lockers with bad words scratched in them, and speckled blue carpet that makes my eyes cross, and everything looks the same as it did when I left.

I came to school the day after Michael died, but I didn't stay. I tried. I really did. I wanted everything to be normal, and on a normal day, I'd be at school. But people already knew about my brother, and they kept giving me this look, like they were wondering when I might snap. When I caught the teacher looking, too, I got up and walked out in the middle of class, kept walking past the double doors and through the courtyard and into the street. It wasn't one of those things that happened. I was calm. I remember it perfectly. I walked all the way across the four-lane and lost myself in the woods for a while. It was the social worker, Grace, who found me, driving up and down the highway in her rickety old Jeep Cherokee. When she picked me up, she ran her fingers through my hair to clean out the pine needles I'd gotten from lying on the ground. She wrapped her sweater around my shoulders. She made me drink some hot coffee from a thermos. That was the day she drove me to Phyllis.

Two class periods and lunch have gone by when I come out of hiding, somewhat more collected now, and aim toward class. I'm still clutching my egg salad sandwiches in their paper sack. In the hall, Anthony Tucker approaches me. It always makes me nervous seeing him approach. There are two versions of Anthony Tucker in my head, the before Chris McKenzie version and the after. Before Chris McKenzie, Anthony could be counted on to snap my bra strap or to jostle me so I dropped my books or to say something rude about my outfit. Ever since he followed me out to the Dumpster that day, he doesn't seem to know what he's supposed to do with me. His solution for a while was to be nice to me, but then his friends noticed, and they started making kissy noises at us, and Anthony went back to proving his dislike for me. Now it's like he's only pretending to be a bully, which is somehow more upsetting than when he was really being mean. Every time he misses the chance to poke me with a pencil or scrape his muddy shoe against my jeans, I think of his face by the Dumpster and I feel like I'm back there for a minute. Anthony tugs at my braid, which is more mess than braid at this point. It's been up for three days. I don't like taking it down. Someone might make me wash my hair.

I can't handle Anthony today. I can't think about how he treats me differently now. I don't speak. I keep walking. Behind me, I hear his buddies making rude noises in time with my steps. I'm afraid they might be following me. I feel like my insides are trembling. I cut half-moons into my palms with my nails. Boys like Anthony Tucker don't understand. They don't know about egg salad on porches, about fists full of dirt that taste like blood. They don't know.

Anthony keeps on and keeps on following, and when he taps me on the shoulder, I'm ready for him. I spin around and punch him in the shoulder as hard as I can.

Except it isn't him; it's the small girl from the bus ride this morning. And instead of her shoulder, I hit her face. She screams. I see blood coming from her nose. I stand perfectly still and will myself backward in time five minutes, but it doesn't work.

The principal calls Phyllis to come get me, even though it's almost time for the buses. I breathe for a minute. Then I ask for the bathroom and find the door instead.

I get on the wrong bus on purpose by writing myself a note from Michael to the bus driver. *Please allow Sasha to take the Cary Fork bus to visit her grandparents. She is to get off at the park.* It shouldn't be this easy to sneak away, but in the chaos of bus boarding, it is. The kids on this bus smell a little better than the ones the Caboose way. Like lotion and chewing gum. Their sneakers look newer. The driver is bored. He barely glances at my note. If there were Greyhound buses here, buses that went to other cities, I'd sneak on one and end up in a faraway city with my clothes stuffed in my backpack and my eyes wide, ready to see new things. I think of how proud that would make Michael.

At the park in the center of Cary Fork, I climb off the school bus and walk as though I know where I'm going. Only once the bus is out of sight do I sag to a stop. Taco Bell is still open, but I didn't bring any money. I eat my sandwiches, which are warm and taste like vinegar and paper bag. I drink the can of soda Phyllis sent with me, which is also warm. I sit on a bench, one of six. There's no caboose here. A bird lands in the grass. I have the girl's blood on my knuckles.

I think about how it would be if I looked up and my mother was there. I am never in Cary Fork. I don't *know* that this isn't where she ran to. I could look up right now and my mother's truck could be there, blue and clean. I'd prefer that she jump out of the truck and run to me, fling her arms around me, grab me, and take me with her. But

I would settle for me chasing after her, getting my hand over the tailgate, which after all these years has a little more rust, and hefting myself into the truck bed. I would lie on my back with the brown pine needles and the flat spare tire until my mother pulled into the driveway of her new home, which would be brick and white and on a hill. When Mom got out of the truck in the circular driveway, I would sit up. I would surprise her.

She would cry. She would apologize for leaving. "I had to get out," she would say. "I was losing my mind, and I had to get out. I've thought about you every day."

I would understand. I mean, I do, sort of. Understand. A little more each day, I feel like I'm losing my mind living in Caboose, where so many bad things have happened, and you only ever see the same things over again: coal-filthy buildings and flood-damaged roads and headlines filled with bad news. I wouldn't have to work hard to understand why she felt like Caboose was a cage she was trapped in.

But I would make her wait before I forgave her.

The inside of the house would be clean. On a shiny oak table inside the door, there would be an iris. Not the part of your eye, but the flower. The walls would all be cream and beige without any Sticky Tack or nail holes. There wouldn't be any streaks on the windows. The carpet would be new and smooth. My gaze would trace the vacuum lines.

It would take me a few nights to forgive her. Once I did, I would crawl into her bed and rest my head on her extra pillow. She would pat her shoulder and open her arms to me, and even though I'm too big to want to cuddle, I would scoot over and do it anyway. She wouldn't smell like Phyllis, like hair spray and dryer sheets. She wouldn't smell like she used to, either, back before she left, when she worked at the Burger Bargain—like grease and weariness. She would smell new. Like soap and flowers and faraway places.

Phyllis arrives shortly after the police car. I don't remember throwing rocks at the streetlights. There is glass on the sidewalk. My mother isn't here.

6

"I would like to get a job," I tell Phyllis.

I'm more comfortable with her now. Comfortable enough to eat at the table at regular hours of the day. Since I've been staying with her, I've more or less figured out her body language, and so far it hasn't told me anything about her being angry with me, like I was afraid of after the guitar. For the most part, she just looks at me like she does her morning crossword, like there are answers she hasn't figured out yet.

We're on the front porch. It's early—not as early as four, but not completely light out, either. It's pouring rain, like it has been for days, and I have to speak up to be heard.

Phyllis waves me quiet with a glance toward the Harless house. Yesterday morning, I forgot not to holler. I woke the babies. The Harless household was not pleased.

"What do you need a job for?" Phyllis asks, soft. Her

voice is like the rain, steady and shushing. Her glasses have slipped down her nose. Her hair isn't in its braid yet and falls loose on her bony shoulders. I've never met anybody as bony as Phyllis, at least not anybody who eats as much egg salad as she does. She tries to wrap up all her bones in broomstick skirts and home-knit shawls, but I can still see her angles.

"I think you're very pretty for an older person," I tell her. I don't know how old she is, but she's old. The middle of her fifties, at least.

"Pffsh, Sasha. What do you need a job for?"

I need money to do what Michael wanted and escape— money for the trip, and money for food and a place to sleep once I get there. But I have to make up the guitar first. I can't leave Phyllis without a guitar and have it be my fault.

"That's private," I tell her.

Phyllis lets out this shaky little breath, and her fingers grip each other and slip off. She worries her thumbs against her forefingers like she's trying to rub off dried glue.

"We have to talk to Grace," she says. "I don't know if jobs are allowed at your age."

"You can call her," I suggest.

"Be nice if you asked," Phyllis points out. Nothing about her is not gentle, but I'm starting to pick up on when I'm testing her patience.

"Would you please call her?" I ask.

"I will."

I wait.

"Not now," Phyllis clarifies. "When it's daylight out, at least."

"I've been thinking," I tell Phyllis. "Maybe I should grow up to be a fireman." Her head whips around sharp, like I've said something shocking. But her voice is steady when she answers.

"That so?"

I finger the too-long sleeves of Michael's Navy sweatshirt I'm wrapped in. I think of Michael's team, his fellow firefighters. How they marched careful patterns at his funeral. How they had his back, even after he died. I don't have family now, but Michael did. I don't necessarily want to fight fires—in fact, I'd like to stay as far away from them as possible. But I'd like to share something with my brother. I'm not making a lot of sense and I know it, so I don't say anything more, but Phyllis keeps going.

"You're too young for that kind of job yet, girl."

"I don't want to work at Burger Bargain."

"You got to be sixteen to work there anyway," she says.

"I don't like the hats. I—" There is too much history to go into, and I stop again, speech grinding into quiet. I focus on the rain to blur out the image of Judy smiling out from under her hat. A quick peck on the cheek and out the door she went, singing her favorite song, "A Bird in a Gilded Cage." I should have listened. I should have

50

realized she was trying to say that *she* felt like a caged bird. Maybe then her flying away wouldn't have shocked me so bad. I don't know if that memory was the day she left, or just any old other day before, but it's the picture in my head.

We sit awhile. Hubert Harless creaks out his front door, kicks one of Mikey's shoes back inside. He locks the door behind him. I raise a hand and he raises one back. I haven't been over again for lunch, but Mikey and I have been staring at each other through the window early every morning. There is something weird about that kid.

This morning, he put his hand flat on the window. I mirrored it with mine. Mine was so big against his small one. I wonder if I was that little at nine. There are days I still feel little. But then I think about how Mikey must feel, and touching hands with him through the window makes me feel bigger and older and stronger.

The next three mornings, Mikey Harless doesn't meet me at the window. I look into his bedroom and see the little girls sleeping in their beds. Sara is two years old, and she is mostly only tangled hair sticking out from under a pillow. Marla is barely a year, and she is chubby feet through the bars of a crib.

Phyllis has told me about the whole family over egg salad sandwiches in our mornings together. I'm fascinated by my coal miner cousin and his apple-scented wife and their trio of kids. Mikey is the most interesting one. Because he's only Hubert's, and because he, as Mr. Powell would describe it, "exhibits unusual behavior," he seems more related to me than his two baby sisters.

According to Phyllis, the Harless clan are decent neighbors, if a little bit odd. Hubert can be counted on to fix the plumbing or the furnace when things go wrong for Phyllis, and he won't accept payment unless it's baked or knitted. Shirley, Phyllis describes as quiet, and she doesn't say much about Mikey—only that he's had a hard time of things. She looks at me too long when she says stuff like that.

I've settled into a routine at school—one that, to Mr. Powell's delight, does not include the regular skipping of classes. I can't keep skipping classes without Grace getting a phone call, and I'm afraid she'll take me from Phyllis. I don't want to leave Phyllis until it's time to leave Caboose.

It's easy to fade into the back of the classroom and not say anything. Only my English teacher seems to want to draw me out, asking me questions in class every chance she gets. I answer as quietly as possible, sometimes only with a shrug or a shake of my head. Her gaze lingers before she moves on to other students. On my persuasive essay assignment against school uniforms, she makes a note in green ink next to one of my better sentences: *This is the sort of thing you ought to say in class! Beautifully put!*

I spend Saturday on Hubert's porch, playing with Marla and Sara. Marla likes to be picked up and spun in circles. She likes to touch faces, pull ears and poke eyes and squeeze noses. I'm constantly untangling her fingers from my hair and trying to keep her from sticking them in my mouth.

Sara does everything Hubert does. Hubert is fixing the porch railing. He lifts a board, and Sara reaches to put her small hand on it, too. Hubert considers the angle of a nail, and Sara tilts her head the same as he does. When Hubert tugs at his beard, Sara tugs at her sharp little chin. When Hubert knocks in a nail with his hammer, Sara chooses a nail that is already driven and smacks it with her bare hand, keeping time.

"I wish the rain would stop," I say to no one. Hubert is fixing the porch rail for the little girls to hold on to, but at this point there's no reason for them to walk down the steps anyway. They'd sink away in the soupy yard.

"Rain ain't bad," he says. Hubert is a guy of few words. I've pestered him all day with questions about himself. About the mine: he drives over to Dogwood every day. About his family: yes, his mother is living—she's over in Elm Fork—but she's ailing and they don't get on good. No, his father isn't living. This is where I stop, not wanting to ask why.

The babies are still dressed for sleep. Sara wears a long T-shirt with the sleeves rolled and rolled and rolled up until she can barely put her arms down over the cuffs. Marla wears a diaper and a pink T-shirt with a glittery LOVE on the front. The weather has suddenly turned spring, warm but wet. Five days of rain have the creek up so high you can see it from the porch, even sitting. Normally you'd have to climb onto the railing to catch a glimpse.

I scoop Sara up and flip her upside down. She shrieks a giggle. Marla's fat hands open and close in the "gimme" signal babies have, so I hook her into the other arm and spin in circles. I go faster with the weight of the babies in my arms. The speed and the weight feel good. The babies squeal.

Hubert puts out his big hands and catches me by the shoulders. I stop spinning, startled. I feel like time has passed. Hubert takes the babies, one under each arm. He looks them both over, but his eyes keep coming back to my face. Eyes crinkled at the corners, mouth disappearing under mustache. He looks so sad, I think I must have missed something.

The babies cling to Hubert. Their cheeks are wet. Marla is wailing. Sara wipes snot off her nose with her too-long sleeve, which has come unrolled and now hangs past her fingertips. "All done!" she sniffles.

I pat the two curly little heads, and then I walk down the steps into the rain. With every step, I test the porch rail, rocking it away from me and back. It doesn't budge like it did before. It holds steady.

"You done a good job," I tell Hubert. I use improper grammar on purpose, to make him feel comfortable.

I'm not at any risk of being hired as a babysitter. But Hubert puts me to work the following week after school, doing odd jobs. You don't need permission to do odd jobs, Phyllis says, and you don't have to be a certain age. It saves her a phone call. I hold boards while Hubert hammers in nails. I lift the screen door into place so he can put in the screws.

"Steady," he says. "Watch your fingers."

"Sorry. I ain't trying to move it, but it's heavy."

The girls are forgiving. They come for kisses. They come for ring-around-the-rosy. Sara wants to be in charge of everything that happens on the porch. She arranges her baby sister like an unwilling rag doll. Marla shakes her off and squalls. Sara gets my hand and tugs me where she wants me. I don't squall. I go where she tugs.

I don't see much of Mikey, though. Once in a while his face pops up in the window I'm washing, and then he darts away and hides under the bed. I can see his filthy feet sticking out.

When I'm not working for my cousin Hubert, squirreling money away for a purchase I need to make, I walk up

West Lane to the pawnshop. The middle of the store is all taken up with jewelry: watches, wedding bands, class rings with old years on them. The edges of the store are music: trumpets, banjos, one harp—and the prettiest guitars I've ever seen.

I strum the strings, and their music makes me think of Phyllis, of the way her singing sounded when I first moved into her house. I wish I'd known her better then. If I knew her better, I'd have sat on my hands. I'd have kept myself under control, no matter what song she sang. Even if it was Judy's song.

I wish I knew how to do more than strum. I think that if I earn enough money working for Hubert Harless, maybe I can buy two guitars, and maybe Phyllis will teach me.

I start thinking of it as a *GUI-tar*, which is how Phyllis says it. I know I can't leave town until she's got one in her hands. Every day when I get off the school bus, I go and stare at the one I want to buy her. Phyllis watches for me from the porch, and every day I tell her a different reason for why the bus was a little late. Traffic. A deer in the road. Stuck behind a tractor.

The first day I was late, she panicked. She called the school. They were already on the radio with the bus driver before I got home, and he assured them he had dropped me off in one piece. After my escape to Cary Fork my first day back at school, Phyllis isn't taking any chances.

But she also doesn't want to meet me at the bus stop, because I told her the other kids will tease me if they see her. A seventh grader is too old to be walked home by a grown-up. The kids at school already think I'm weird, with my visits to Mr. Powell and my history of violence. Getting picked up at the bus stop like I can't find my own way home would be the last straw.

The GUI-tar I've picked out for Phyllis looks a lot like her old one, but it's shinier. I've looked at the price tag several times, willing the numbers to get smaller. I've also tried staring squint-eyed at my cousin, willing the money he pays me to get bigger.

"You having eye trouble?" he asks.

It's going to be a while before Phyllis has a GUI-tar.

I'm a little worried, anyway, that when she gets it, she won't want to play it anymore. At least not when I'm around. But I can only fix one problem at a time.

7

Spring comes to Caboose in patches.
First, there are three or four days at a time of warm
weather, followed by snowstorms that keep my pockets
fat from all the walkways I'm shoveling for Hubert. The
April weather is all mixed up. There are flower petals scattered across snow while thunder rumbles over the mountains, like the weather just can't make up its mind what
season to be. For the most part, I'm settling in at Phyllis's,
but my moods are a lot like the weather. Some days I'm
springtime warm and hopeful, lying on the porch with
the sun on my face. Other days, grief for Michael blows
through me like a cold wind, thundering for me to go, to
get out, to *move*.

The first summer-warm day comes on a Thursday in
April, too early to be convincing, but welcome anyway.
It's over eighty and so nice that they ought to let us skip

school to enjoy it, but no such luck. I'm looking forward to a quick stop at the pawnshop and a long afternoon on the porch, but on the school bus, I start hearing whispers about why there's extra traffic in and out of Caboose. Kids are on their phones and looking online, passing stories back and forth. Nobody talks to me, but I don't have to be popular to pick up on the word *accident*. Despite the weather, I rub my hands up and down my arms to chase away the chill.

I skip the pawnshop, and by the time I've made it a quarter mile from the bus stop, I'm jogging. Hubert's home early, just pulling in as I make it to the driveway. I stand on the porch and watch my cousin go in. He slams his truck door and roars a curse when the seat belt jams in the door. On his way up the steps, he kicks the porch railing and knocks loose one of the sturdy nails we just put in. I can't help thinking he's never quite looked so kin to me as he does right now.

He disappears inside without so much as a glance my way. I watch his screen door slam shut with a bounce before I head into Phyllis's house. She's standing in front of the TV, in the middle of the living room, even though she's not two paces from a chair.

"Oh," she says when she sees me. "It's already time for you?" Her smile doesn't reach her eyes, which stray back to the TV after only a second.

The man on TV is talking about an accident at the

Dogwood mine. He talks about how many things we don't know yet: how many miners, and whether they're hurt or worse than that. He doesn't seem to know much of anything for sure. His cameraman angles toward flashing lights all clustered on the gravel road that leads out to Dogwood. You can't see past the fence.

"It's terrible," Phyllis says. She makes a noise with her mouth, the same one she made the day I broke her guitar. "Just terrible. Almighty."

I think of Ben. I hurt. "Did people die in the mine today?" Like there's a chance she knows something more than the TV guy.

"They ain't told us yet, Sasha."

The man on TV dressed better than any of the men he's praying for. I picture the view from *his* neighbor's porch. The door would open and a serious-looking man in a suit would walk out. No scrub-brush beard. No friendly wave. No tripping over baby shoes. No coveralls. He probably doesn't even come out of his house before eight. If he were my neighbor, I would leave for school every day without ever seeing him.

I think about Hubert, about how we were supposed to work on cleaning the outbuilding today. I wonder if the Dogwood mine is going to close. If it closes, Hubert won't have any place to work. He might not be able to pay me, and then I'll never be able to afford a GUI-tar for Phyllis.

"I hope Hubert doesn't lose his job," I say.

"Lord above, *Hubert*," Phyllis whispers, without taking her eyes off the screen.

"He looked mad when he came in," I say.

Her head whips around. "He's home?"

"He came in cussing from the truck. Just now."

"God Almighty." She sinks into her rocker, lifts herself back up, and swipes her knitting yarn out of the seat before sinking down again. "God Almighty."

The TV is showing footage now from somebody's shaky cell phone camera. There is sunshine. There are flashing fire-truck lights. I stare and stare at the fire-truck lights. In front of them, a woman with her hair in a messy bun says her husband didn't want to go back to the mines, not after the big collapse. She doesn't have to explain, because we all know she means five years ago; we all know she means Hardwater, the collapse that killed Ben. She says her husband wanted to take classes on how to fix computers, but they had bills. They had babies. He didn't have that freedom. She twists and twists her hands. She says she's holding out hope.

The camera cuts back to the man in the suit. He shakes his head slowly. His mouth tightens into a straight line. "We're all holding out hope," he says, without a speck of hope anywhere in his voice. He sounds like he already knows he's going to be reporting a different headline in a day or two, one without any hope left. Across the screen, red block letters pop up, in case anybody's just tuning in: THREE WEST VIRGINIA MINERS TRAPPED BENEATH GROUND.

And over his shoulder, the flag, and on it, our state motto: *Montani Semper Liberi*. Mountaineers are always free.

8

Me and Michael stayed up so late that Tuesday that Wednesday came and we were still on the couch.

"Michael?" The TV was on, had been on for hours, but my voice still sounded loud in the room.

"What." He was distracted, didn't even look at me, and there was no question in his voice. I wasn't sure he even realized I was talking, so I wrapped my fingers around his forearm.

"Michael."

Now he forced his throat clear as he turned to look at me. We hadn't bothered turning on the overheads, and in the dim light from the TV, his face looked lined and tired, shining with sweat. He looked older than I'd ever seen him look. "What, Lightbulb?" His childhood nickname for me, because I had so many bad ideas, like dropping glass dishes or dressing up the cat.

Now that I had his attention, I couldn't remember what my question was. Maybe I didn't have one at all. Maybe the silence was getting to me and I needed his attention, even if I didn't have anything to say. I swallowed, pinned by his painful gaze.

"Can I stay home from school today?"

He laughed a little, a sad laugh like he didn't understand the question. "Yeah," he said. "Yeah, let's, uh . . . let's stay home and clean up the place, huh?"

We did. We cleaned every last inch of the apartment. Michael vacuumed while I scrubbed down the baseboards. While he washed the dishes, I dusted each individual book on the shelf. I shined the windowpanes while my brother scrubbed the toilet. By the time the sun rose, there was no shortage of sparkling-clean surfaces for it to reflect off of. It made the whole place feel strange.

"Michael?" I asked.

He swallowed hard. "What?" This time I got the sense he was paying attention to me, so much attention that I couldn't spit out my original question. I didn't ask about our father. I didn't ask what on earth we would do if he really wasn't coming home.

"Can I stay home tomorrow, too?" I asked instead.

He shook his head as he slowly sank back into the couch, gaze finding the TV, where the same headlines cycled again and again, telling us nothing. A map flickered to life, highlighting where our county was in relation to the rest of the *state. Not everybody, even within West Virginia, knew we were down here, with our abandoned buildings and our single source of income.*

"No, baby. You have to go back to school tomorrow. You have to get out of this place." I didn't know whether he meant our apartment or our town, and I didn't ask.

I don't remember deciding to walk from Phyllis's house to me and Michael's apartment in the middle of the night. It's after one. I ought to be sleeping. I sort of wander down the stairs, and once I'm down the stairs, it's easy to wander out the door, and once I'm out the door, my feet choose a direction. *You have to get out of this place.* My feet speed up, and gravel rolls under my feet. It's dark, and the weather has snapped back to cold. The sky is heavy with clouds, and in the glow of each streetlight, I can see my breath for a minute before I plunge back into the dark. Snowflakes cluster under each light, not seeming to fall, only floating in cold clouds. It's late for snow. From somewhere in my memory, I call up Michael's term for April snow: *blackberry winter*. The berries are supposed to grow sweeter if you get a good snow in April.

Caboose is dead quiet at this hour, but even dead-quiet towns have life. Somebody's dog is barking, and from one or two windows, I catch a glimmer of TV light. I like the way my bare feet sound on the gravel by the highway. The soft crunch is earthy and it calms me down. I feel like I'm okay here, as long as I don't stop moving, as long as I never stop moving.

I end up at home, or at what once was my home. Our apartment was the top floor of this brick house. Although the first-floor windows are dark, I can tell there are still people living behind them. There are curtains and, beyond them, the soft glow of a bathroom light left on. It makes the upstairs windows look even lonelier, curtainless and completely dark.

I let myself in through the back fence, the door the trash men use to empty the Dumpsters. This was the way I used to get in any time I forgot my key, which was once or twice a week. From the fire escape, I climb to the top floor and slide open the window with the broken lock. Without any groceries on the counter or dirty dishes in the sink, the kitchen doesn't feel as familiar as I thought it would. I cross to the light switch, bare feet on ice-cold linoleum. The light switch doesn't work, of course—nobody's been paying any of the bills; nobody lives in this apartment—and fear creeps into my belly at being alone in the dark. My footfalls echo until it sounds like I'm not the only one walking.

The place is filthy like we left it. Boot prints track up the kitchen floor, and the sink is stained from dirty dishes and rust-colored water. I try the faucets, but they won't turn on, of course. There isn't any water, just like there isn't any light. I do the best I can with what I have, which is half a roll of paper towels from under the sink and my own spit. I scrub the sink, scrape at the dried boot prints until some of the marks lift away. I use the bottom of my shirt to wipe the windows, but they stay grimy and I can't see much on the other side.

When it starts to get light out, I stop cleaning and head back to Phyllis's. Although I haven't slept, I feel like somebody waking up after a nap they didn't mean to take. I try to hurry, but people in cars still stare at a jogging girl in her pajamas with no coat on. Two different times, someone stops to help. When they pull over, I walk faster. Then a police car pulls over. I stop. My heart hits the back of my rib cage faster and faster.

Phyllis is trying to hide tears when I get out of the police car. I'm washed in guilt. She runs to me, reaches out like she's going to hug me or slap me—I can't tell which, because her hands are shaking. Either way, she stops short. She keeps shoving bits of gray hair behind her ears. I think she's gotten grayer in the two months we've known each other. She thanks the officer, who speaks quietly with her. She hurries me inside, where there is oatmeal and blankets.

"Phyllis?"

"Hmm?" She's cleaning the kitchen again, washing out oatmeal bowls while I soak my feet in a hot pan of water. The water's murky and gray from all the filth I picked up along the road, but my feet feel thawed.

"Can I stay home today?" It feels like weeks have passed since Thursday, but somehow it's only Friday. The clock on the oven, right again now that it's spring, says I'm going to be late for the bus if I don't leave soon.

Phyllis pulls a spoon from the drainer and holds it up to the light, then runs it under water again. It isn't until she's rubbing it dry with a dish towel that she answers, "I wish you would."

The snow comes back at dusk. The flakes are small and beady against the heavy, wet gray of the sky. I sit in bed and think about how I didn't visit the GUI-tar today. It seems far away, like my life before Michael died.

Phyllis sits on the edge of my bed, picking at one corner of the blanket.

"Sasha, tell me what you need," she says. "Tell me what on this earth'll keep you from running off like this." Her voice is not her usual Sasha voice. It's the kind of voice people use to plead with traffic to move out of their way, or to plead with God to make somebody stay. It's the kind of voice people use when they're not really talking to the person right in front of them.

I don't know what I need. I need time to slow down. I need to escape Caboose, or I need to stop feeling like I'm going to lose my mind if I don't. I stay quiet, playing with the bits of yarn sticking up out of the center of each quilt square. We play with opposite ends of our blanket, me and Phyllis. I can hear the wind playing with the loose shingles on Hubert's roof. A siren starts up somewhere out in the town.

Phyllis blows out a breath. I think about how I'm not hers and about how everybody has to have a giving-up point. I can't look at her anymore, at the eyes I've made sad and the hands I've made shake. Guilt and dread make me weak, and I sink down under the covers, rolling away from her. I tug up the quilt. It smells like laundry detergent. I feel it slip from her grasp when I pull.

"Wake me," she says, and now her voice is closer to the one I'm used to hearing. "Before you go running off again, just . . . just *wake* me. Then if you still have to run, I'll run with you." She rests the back of her warm hand against my cheek for a long moment, but she doesn't kiss me good night.

9

For two days, I'm too sick to realize
I'm sick. I try to lie perfectly still, and I wonder why the room is spinning. Sometimes Phyllis is there with oatmeal or soup or tea I can't drink. Sometimes I'm alone in the room and I keep thinking I'm seeing things move in the dark corners.

By the time I wake on Monday, there's news I don't want to hear coming in from the mines, so I'm sick in another way. I stay under the covers.

The blankets and sheets don't smell like laundry detergent anymore. They smell like sweat and sickness and me. On Wednesday, the first of May, I feel well enough to escape them. I make my shaky way out to the porch. The world looks wet, like it's been raining, but it's much warmer than it was when I was last out. Weak evening sun turns the porch boards orange, even though I know they're chipped-paint gray.

I'm not expecting to see Hubert. He should be in for supper about now. But his screen door creaks open almost as soon as I sit down.

He doesn't look like himself in his suit. His hair is slicked back with visible comb streaks, and he keeps tugging at his necktie. Although his outfit matches the ones the news anchors have been wearing on TV, Hubert doesn't in any way look like those men. He looks uncomfortable and sweaty.

"Hi," I call, raising a hand.

He raises one back. "Feeling better, little lady?"

I smile a little. Ben used to call me that, too. "Yep." I study him. He looks so different today. Behind him, Shirley comes out of the house in a black dress. She's got Marla in her arms, and Sara toddles beside them. Both little girls are in dark dresses, Sara's green and Marla's blue. Marla is fussing and bending over her mother's arm. She wants down to play. But Shirley must know as well as I do that if she puts Marla down, the baby will go immediately to the muddiest place she can find and the dress will be ruined.

Sara opens and closes her hands in a baby wave, and I wave back. I watch the door behind her. When Mikey comes out, he's wearing a suit like his father's. His hair is so gelled it looks like a solid thing. His face is red and tear-streaked, and I feel a pang of sympathy for him.

"It's a prayer vigil," Hubert's saying as Mikey follows him down the steps. "You can't wear sneakers to a prayer vigil, son. I'm sorry."

"We're taking the car," Shirley says when Mikey darts past her to his father's pickup.

"I will rot in hell before I ride in that car!" These are the first words I have ever heard Mikey say.

"Mikey," his father warns. It's been a long time since I've had a father, but I had a big brother recently enough that I recognize that tone of voice. I figure Mikey ought to listen.

But he doesn't. "If you try to make me go in Shirley's car, I'll die and I'll rot in hell and then you'll have to get dressed up and go to *my* funeral!"

"William Michael Harless!" I'm relieved to learn that Mikey is his middle name. I want *my* Michael to be the *only* Michael. When Hubert speaks again, his voice has already lowered. "Please get in the car."

Mikey backs away, shaking his head. His chin is high. I sit up straighter. Something about how stiffly he's holding his shoulders, something about the way he keeps shaking his head, is familiar. I can feel it in my own chin, in my own bones. All at once, I have an opinion on the situation next door.

"He can stay with me," I call.

Mikey's head whips around so fast his gelled hair moves an inch. "I don't know you," he says. But he doesn't sound quite as fierce as before.

"I'm Sasha," I explain, although I'm sure he knows at least that. "Your father's father and my father's father were brothers. That makes us . . . something. Some sort of cousins. First cousins twice removed."

"Second cousins," Hubert corrects. "You and I are first cousins once removed. You and Mikey are second cousins."

"See? I'm your cousin. Hubert says."

Mikey studies me for a long moment. Then he nods.

"Guess I'll stay, then." Like he's doing me a favor.

Phyllis is trying to teach us to cook.

"You could stand to eat something more solid than egg salad and oatmeal," she tells me.

"But why can't you just cook it?"

"Because." She points to the sink. I wash my hands, with a lot of soap because I know she's watching. Mikey shuffles in behind me. He's taken off the tie and the jacket. Now he's only wearing an undershirt. It looks weird with his black slacks and bare feet. Mikey has black road dirt tattooed on his feet the way Hubert's hands wear permanent coal dust. I wonder how long it took Hubert to get shoes on him.

"*Because* is not an answer," I say, echoing my English teacher. Phyllis flips the dish towel at me. The first time she did this, I wasn't sure what she meant by it. Ben and Judy weren't the dish-towel-flipping type. I wasn't sure if having a dish towel flipped at me was a good thing or a bad thing. Since then, I've figured out that it's one of the ways Phyllis teases me, like when she tugs my braid or when she calls me "Sasha Serious." Phyllis doesn't tease the way Anthony does. With Phyllis, it's all right.

"Are you sure this is a good idea?" I ask when it looks like Phyllis is getting down to business about this cooking thing. When I was little, my parents worked so much that we mostly ate dinners Judy brought home from the Burger Bargain. Then when I got older, and it was just me and Ben and Michael, Michael did all the cooking, and he didn't always have the patience to teach me. Later, when me and Michael were alone in the first little house we shared, we didn't have a good working kitchen. And by the time we moved to the apartment, I'd done enough stupid things just with the microwave and hot plate that Michael didn't really want me anywhere near an actual stove. Not with him seeing the things he saw from the fire truck on a weekly basis.

Phyllis says we're going to cook muffins with anything we want in them. "Not *anything*," she stops herself. "Y'all two, who knows what you'd throw in there. You can have walnuts, chocolate chips, or strawberries. That's all I've got that would make sense in muffins."

"Yes, please," I say. Mikey nods his approval.

"All three, then." She sets them one by one on the counter, then begins whipping around the kitchen so quickly I'm sure I'm going to be knocked on the head by a cabinet door.

"Where's the recipe?" I ask, retreating to safety near the sink. I pull Mikey with me so he won't be killed. He is mostly bone and empty space and he pulls easily. He looks taller today than usual with his dark hair standing stiff. His face is all cheekbone and freckle. He actually looks a lot like me.

"Pffsh," Phyllis says. She whips out a mixing bowl and a measuring cup. "Preheat the oven to three fifty."

"I don't know how to do that."

With a twitch of her eyebrow, Phyllis shows me how to spin the dial. At the last minute, she remembers to pull the pizza pans out of the oven, where they've been stored.

"Wash your hands again," Phyllis instructs. "You've been playing with your hair." My hair is on day two of a braid. It's nearly all frizz at this point, the core of the braid hidden by loose tangles. The rubber band at the bottom is barely hanging on.

I wash my hands again. Phyllis isn't watching as closely, so I don't use as much soap.

"When you're finished, you can grease the tin," she tells me.

"I don't know how to do that."

"Oh, for heaven's sake." Phyllis puts down the bowl

she's been drying and crosses to me. "How you have made it this far in life is beyond me, girl . . ." Her voice fades out, but she's still muttering under her breath. I catch something about "kids today" and I tune out.

Mikey steps in before Phyllis can take over my job. "*I* know," he says. He shows me how to smear butter all over the muffin tin. "My mom taught me all about cooking. Now your muffins won't stick," he explains. "If you don't do this part, everything sticks to the tin, and when you pick up a muffin, you only get the top. Shirley uses cooking spray, but it doesn't taste as good. She and Dad got in a fight about it once."

"That's a weird thing to get in a fight over," I say.

"Shirley and my dad get in fights over a lot of weird stuff."

"I need a measurer and a mixer," Phyllis says. "Any takers?"

I eye the mixing bowl with concern. "This is the part where the wheels tend to come off the wagon," I tell her. I'm thinking of the time I tried to make dinner for Michael and the kitchen ended up splattered in raw eggs.

"You didn't know how to preheat the oven or grease a muffin tin, and *this* is the part where the wheels tend to come off the wagon?"

"Well, there are a lot of wheels on a wagon," I tell her. "More than one can come off."

Mikey cracks up laughing and drops the measuring cup.

• • •

We sing while we wait for the muffins. Mikey has cheered up a lot. I've heard him described as a handful, and half the reason I invited him over was morbid curiosity, to find out how much of a handful he is. But so far he's measured ingredients and helped wash the dishes. He has, without being told, wiped down the table with a dishrag, which never would have occurred to me. He already knows the words to half of Phyllis's songs. Sure, he's got a colorful vocabulary. But overall, Mikey seems a lot less of a handful than me.

We eat muffins and watch a scary movie on cable. Phyllis gasps every time a fake zombie jumps out, and I have to explain how you can tell they're fake, not just because I don't think zombies really exist, but also because you can see the makeup lines.

"That's not true!" Mikey says. He's got melted chocolate chips smeared all over his face, and strawberries down the front of his shirt. "Real zombies have makeup lines just to fool you into thinking they're fake zombies! Then when you lean in to ask, 'Is this CoverGirl or Maybelline?'— that's the two kinds of makeup Shirley uses to chase *her* zombie face away—that's when they pounce and rip your face off and . . . and bake it into muffins!"

"Don't tell her that; now she'll never eat one!" Phyllis

swats him lightly. "And don't talk about your stepmom that way!" Then she asks me, "Why don't you try a bite? It won't bite you back!" She's eaten half a muffin already. Mikey's on his third. I've been picking the walnuts out of mine, because I changed my mind about them.

"The walnuts look a little grosser than I thought they would," I explain. "I can sort of picture these being zombie muffins. The walnuts could be . . . gnarled finger bones."

Mikey nods seriously. "That's true. My mom said you never know where something scary will turn up. That's why you have to keep your eye out. Even with muffins."

"Bite," Phyllis repeats. She has this look on her face that lets us know she's listening to Mikey, even though she doesn't answer.

I try a bite. The muffins are warm from the oven, and the chocolate chips are melty. It's a little like biting into . . . I can't think of any way to say it, because I've never bit into anything that tasted this good.

"So what's the verdict?" Phyllis asks.

"The most delicious gnarled finger bones I've ever tasted," I admit.

By the time the zombies and their gnarled fingers have gone off the TV, I've eaten four muffins and I'm almost asleep. I've leaned so far sideways on Phyllis's couch that Stella is using my stomach as a bed. She purrs on and off between catnaps. I don't really care for cats, but the warmth is nice.

Mikey is passed out on the rug with an arm looped over Chip, like he's a teddy bear. We let the animals in a while ago because the road outside will be clogged with cars again once the prayer vigil is over. It's not a funeral. Those will be later, and private. It's just a gathering, a chance for people to be together and to say good-bye. I've been to them before. They're better than funerals—there are still flowers, but no shiny boxes—but still, I'm grateful to be here instead.

Phyllis gets up and takes our leftover muffins to the kitchen. I hear her moving around in there, creaking the linoleum and closing the refrigerator. She comes back with her last cup of coffee and sits. I think she thinks I'm asleep, because she doesn't speak. She pats my knee.

She changes the channel to the news, which she always has to watch before bed in case anybody she knows is on it. Phyllis is a worrier. I figure it's all the coffee.

I let my eyes close. The TV newsman is talking about a car accident in Rathbone. Then there's a drug bust in Jane. Then he says *Caboose*. I open my eyes again.

There it is, on TV. The vigil. The flowers. The newsman's voice is sugar-sweet sad. He talks about the two miners from Caboose. He says the other one lived over in Bent Tree. He was only nineteen. He was a Red Hat in training. He was only six years older than me.

The newsman talks about the lives of the miners, and that's what he calls them the whole time: *miners*. As though that were the main thing about them.

Five years ago, I stood at Ben's service. I remember them calling Ben a miner. I remember them saying it over and over: *God bless these lost miners. Jesus is waiting to welcome them to Heaven.* I remember thinking how Ben was a dad and a husband and a cardplayer and he liked to eat pizza toppings but not the crust and he liked to watch the second ten minutes of the news but not the first, because he didn't want us kids to see the worst parts. I remember wondering why they had to pick that one thing, the mining, to talk about at his funeral. Sure, he ran a machine that dug coal out of the ground. He climbed deep into tunnels with low ceilings, and he made more money for his company than anybody, some days. But then he came home. He called me his "Sasha Love" and said I was his bright spot. He looked tired all the time. He read two books before bed, one to me and one to himself. He was made out of other stuff besides the coal mine.

I can't watch the news anymore. I cuddle Stella to my face and try to sleep. Only now that Ben's in my head, I can't shake him back loose again. I'm halfway in between asleep and awake, aware of the pattern of the fabric of Phyllis's sofa pressing into my cheek, but also feeling Ben's hands there, the way he used to pat my face, leaving streaks of filth from work. Ben was more affectionate than a lot of dads in Caboose, and even more so after Judy left. He made it a habit to squeeze and hug and pat and lift and spin. Since his death, nobody has ever hugged me so tight. Michael mostly kept his arms at his sides, or loosely draped across the back of the sofa, or fixed to the ladder of the fire truck.

I'm not done missing Ben, and now I've started up with missing Michael, too. I'm missing him elbowing me and calling me "Beanpole" and "Lightbulb." I'm missing him pressing and pressing for me to go off to college, to go someplace else. I'm missing those few hugs I did get from him, how carefully he held me and how safe he made me feel. I squeeze Stella tighter, breathe against her warm fur. I wish Phyllis would pat my knee again. I think about Hubert, the closest relative I've got anymore. I wonder if he's the hugging type and maybe he just doesn't know me well enough yet to hug. Or maybe it's me. Maybe I'm not the kind of person who looks like you can hug her.

Hubert comes in late to retrieve Mikey. The two of them, one sad and one sleepy, make their way out of Phyllis's house. I stretch and head up to my room. Now that I've napped, I feel wide awake, not ready to climb into bed yet. I look around.

It surprises me to realize that the room doesn't look

like I live here. Most of my treasures still live in the suit-case under the bed, ready to run if I get half a chance.

Today, I learned how to cook something. And today, I fell asleep safe, knowing Phyllis was there to watch out for me.

I pull out the suitcase and undo the clasps. The GUI-tar money is stashed away on one side, along with my small wad of escape money. I know it isn't near enough for col-lege, but I've only been saving for a couple of years. It would have been enough to help me with a train ticket or a plane ride. Now it's going to help me replace Phyllis's GUI-tar.

I take the old picture of me and Michael out of the suitcase and hold it close for a minute. It's ruined from the day I tried to run away in the rain. You can't even tell who's in it, but I know. I place it on the top of the dresser, which has stayed empty the whole time I've been here. Beside it, I place a handful of rocks—one glittery rock Judy gave me that she called fool's gold, one piece of hard black coal from Ben's mine, and one smooth river rock that Michael called a worry stone. Beside the rocks, I place a small stack of photos, facedown. I like having them close, but I'm not ready to look at them yet.

Now the only thing left in the suitcase is my notebook. In its pages, I've kept track of ideas for how to escape Caboose. They all involve Michael. I've written down fire-fighter jobs in other cities that I found online. I've written down a list of colleges with family housing, so he can take me with him. I've researched scholarships and grants and student loans for him.

I was going to tell him all about it. Soon. As soon as I had it all figured out.

Now that Michael is gone, I don't know what to do with the notebook. I'm too young to get any of the jobs that he could have gotten. I'm too young for college. I can't take out any loans. It's going to be a while now before I manage to find a way to escape Caboose.

But I have to do it. Even more so now that Michael's gone, I can feel how this town might drain me away. I'm tired and sad like all the grown-ups here. I don't want to get stuck like Michael did, like he always feared I would.

I hold the notebook for a long time. It's one thing to decide to stay with Phyllis for a while. It's another to trust her with my notebook. It goes back in the suitcase, and I clasp the lid closed.

10

Nine and nineteen, we walked uptown one bright morning, with heavy sun streaming down like a tall glass of something sweet. My legs weren't as long as Michael's and I got tired before he did, but it took me blocks to be willing to admit it. By the time I did, I was so tired that I didn't warn Michael before plopping onto the porch of one of the abandoned buildings by the side of the road. There were handfuls of them all along Route 10 for as long as I could remember. I thought I could remember this building being a feed and hardware store once. I remembered a bin labeled "Penny Candy," only the sweets cost a dollar. It was tough to tell what the worn-down lettering on the glass used to say.

We sat the longest time without talking. That was how it was with me and Michael. We didn't always have to talk. He was tired, too. He'd worked all day at his firefighter gig and late into the night over at the Save-Great. He smelled like smoke and spoiled milk. He hadn't talked about the Navy in a long time.

"Listen here," he said. "I know you think I've been on you too hard about that spelling test."

I shifted on the porch boards, embarrassed. I didn't like him being disappointed in me. It wasn't that I hadn't studied, exactly. I had. At least, I looked over the words once, on the bus ride to school.

"It was just a Friday test. It hardly counts."

"Everything counts." He leveled this stern look at me that made me think of our mother. "Everything you learn now is going to help you get where you want to go in life."

Anytime a grown-up said something like "where you want to go in life," I tuned out, but this time, Michael wouldn't let me. He had that look on his face again, the one he only wore when big things went wrong. But all he said was, "You're going to go someplace."

I felt warm and sleepy, and I didn't really feel like going anywhere. "Where we going?" I asked.

"Just somewhere." His sigh was short and didn't sound quite like him. "People grow up here and they . . . they get stuck, Sash. They get tired and they get in a rut, and then before they know it, they're thirty and nothing's ever gonna change. There's a whole world out there, and most people here, they don't ever see it."

I looked up the road at the sun splashing patterns on the pavement. Yellow flowers sprouted out of cracks in the sidewalk. "Ain't this part of the world?"

"Ain't *ain't* a word, squirt. And yeah, this is part. Only it's just *one* part. You've got to promise me you're going to see at least a few of the other parts. The better ones." His voice went low, almost like he wasn't even talking to me anymore. "I can't stand the thought of you staying in this damn town your whole life."

I thought of our mother, who ran away, and I linked my arm through Michael's, suddenly scared he might disappear, too. It wasn't till a long time later, thinking back, that I realized that was around the time Michael stopped talking about getting himself out of here. The only escape he talked about anymore was mine.

I sit alone on the bus every day. It's funny how people leave room around you once they know you as "that kid who punched that other kid for no reason." But once I'm in my seat the morning after the vigil, the girl I punched changes seats to slide in next to me.

This is such a shock that it takes me a moment to process. By the time I have, she's already making herself at home on the far end of the bench seat, slipping out of her backpack straps and balancing the pack on her skinny knees.

"Hi," she says. Her voice, like her hair and the tip of her nose, defies gravity, lilting upward. I try to think of an appropriate response. One that convinces her how sorry I am to have punched her. One that explains it was an accident. One that buys me a fresh start.

I come up with, "Hi."

"I wasn't"—except she pronounces it like *wadn't*—"sure you wanted any friends, but I never noticed you having any and I thought"—except she pronounces it like *thowt*—"you might be looking for one."

"Well, that's . . ." I search for something I can say that will match her manner of speaking and make her feel comfortable. I end up saying, ". . . hmm."

We sit while the trees hop by. I say *hop* because the bus is bouncing. Road crews never make it this far out the holler.

"We got nine goats and five cats, but I ain't allowed to get a dog," she tells me.

"You moved here with nine goats and five cats? How'd that work?"

"We didn't move. I just never came to school before."

This doesn't sound possible. "How'd you manage that?"

"I was homeschooled. But now my dad thinks I need more social skills."

She seems plenty social to me, but then my standards in that area are low.

"I'm Jaina," she offers.

Even though I already know this—everybody knows the new kid's name—I pounce on the new topic. "I'm Sasha."

"I know," she says. Then she looks embarrassed. I shouldn't be surprised she knows my name. Everybody knows the weird kid, too.

In social studies, we do coal mining as a current event. It's not one of the lessons they made us write down in our planners, and I remind myself that I shouldn't complain to Mr. Powell about it later. I hate when the teachers don't stay on topic. It's easier to talk about classwork than real stuff. But Mr. Powell has told me more than once that my constant critique of my classes has more to do with me needing to feel in control than it does with my education. He says it's because so many things have been out of my control lately.

It's not that I don't see his point. It's just that it's really not what we'd had planned for today, and for once, I had my homework done.

Also, I really don't like to talk about coal mining.

Talking about coal mining in Caboose never ends well. It's been brought up more and more lately because of a few big accidents in our own state as well as in Kentucky, Tennessee, and other places that share our livelihood. When people run for office, they talk about it, and then everybody at home talks about it. How accident rates really are on the decline, and the news just makes it seem otherwise. How so-and-so's daddy and his daddy and his daddy were coal miners and it was good enough for them. How it's the best living around and how politicians care more about the environment than jobs.

Today's class discussion goes a little bit different. It seems like everybody in class knows somebody who knows somebody who knew the miners who died last week.

"But it was a freak accident," one kid says. "It's a dangerous job; that's one reason they get paid so much. They know it's dangerous. That's what they sign up for."

"I think what they sign up for is having a job, period," a boy in the front row offers. "The other stuff they just have to put up with."

"Your dad owns a laundry mat!" the first kid points out, distracted, pulling her hair up into a ponytail while she argues. "My dad and uncle are miners, and they love what they do! They're not 'just putting up with' anything!"

"There's a lot of jobs that's dangerous!" another boy pipes up. "Police, paramedics, firemen . . ." His voice trails off, and I sense the second when half the people in the class glance at me.

I raise my hand.

"Sasha?" Mr. Pope asks. "You can speak up. You don't have to raise your hand during current events."

I slowly withdraw my hand, keeping my head down.

"May I be excused? I'd like to talk to Mr. Powell, if that's all right."

But I don't. I sit in his office, drawing treetops on the inside cover of my social studies books. Treetops are easy. They're all leaves and smudgy texture. It's the trunks that give me trouble. I can't ever get the angle right.

Mr. Powell finishes with the student before me, a burly kid with a wallet chain hanging out of his pocket, legs the width of the tree trunks I've been drawing, disappearing sockless into untied kicks. My eyes trail from his retreating figure to Mr. Powell standing in the doorway of his office.

"Ms. Harless," he says. "To what do I owe the pleasure?"

"Social studies," I answer.

He sighs shortly. "Come in."

"No, thanks."

"Sasha, you came to see me." He's moving quickly through the stages of Mr. Powell anxiety. He started out with his hands at his sides, but now they've moved to his pockets. He bounces up onto the balls of his feet and back down.

"Yeah, but you were busy. Now the bell's about to ring."

He walks out to sit next to me in the yellow fabric-covered chairs that line the rose-pink wall. His hands go from pockets to running through his thick hair right on schedule. "Sasha. Is everything all right?"

I glance up from my drawing. "I mean, I don't want to be late for English."

Right on time, his arms crisscross his chest. I've gotten pretty good at reading Mr. Powell's frustration with me. "Why didn't you want to stay in social studies?"

I glance back down at my book and start erasing the treetops before he can get mad about them. I don't know what to say.

"Were they discussing something that was upsetting to you?"

Bingo! But I don't tell him that. The more times Mr. Powell is right, the more times I think there might actually be something wrong with me.

"Were they discussing yesterday's candlelight vigil?"

I think of the flowers on the news. The stories that couldn't begin to sum up what the stories left behind had lost. I smack the cover of my book shut, hard.

"We weren't supposed to talk about it!" I blurt out, and then the bell rings.

In English we do haiku. Five syllables in the first line, seven in the second, and five again in the last. They're supposed to have something to do with nature, like running streams or hazy mountains. They're supposed to capture a single moment in time.

We're supposed to do three. The kids around me moan

and groan. Something about the shortness of haiku feels good to my pencil. I write and write.

I do:

Walking from the store
where the GUI-tar waits for me—
when will it be ours?

I do:

Mom picked up and left.
The rest of us waited, but
she didn't come back.

I do:

Mom sang about birds.
No, that isn't quite true. She
sang about cages.

I do:

Dad walked down and down.
Me and Michael waited, but
he didn't come back.

I do:

> Phyllis likes to sing,
> but guitars will break when they
> hit the windowpane.

I do:

> On the bus today,
> Jaina sat and talked to me.
> Could we become friends?

I do:

> Coal mines can collapse.
> I watch miners come and go—
> except when they die.

I do:

> So many people
> are down under the ground here.
> Some in mines. Some not.

We read our haiku to the class, each student choosing one to share. We hear poems about report cards and poems about cardinals on tree branches and poems about how much the writer doesn't like writing poetry. I can't imagine how I'm going to choose just one. I finally do:

> In history class,
> we do a lot of talking
> about scary things.

Miss Jacks calls me to her desk after class. "Sasha," she says. "I wanted to talk to you about your poems." She's holding my paper in her hand.

"I know they're supposed to be about nature," I blurt, afraid she's going to give me a bad grade. Michael always said I have to get good grades if I want someone else to pay for college. *And believe me, sister, you want somebody else to pay for college.*

Miss Jacks wears T-shirts and jeans instead of the khakis and polos most of the other teachers wear. Today's T-shirt is sky blue and says GRIZZLIES on it, showing our school mascot. She's got long brown hair that she wears loose on her shoulders so that it tangles around the stems of her glasses; she's always having to take them off and sort them out.

She's looking at me with this long, strange look that I've

never seen on a teacher's face before. Like she's afraid of me or something. "They *are* about nature, Sasha," she says. "They're about the nature of where you're growing up."

Or maybe not afraid *of* me so much as *for* me. I don't know what to say, so I look at the clock and then the door.

"You're an excellent student," she says. "Just like your brother."

No one's ever called me an excellent student before, but I'm more interested in the second thing she said. "You had Michael?"

"Twice. Honors and yearbook. He was a brilliant student, your brother. A beautiful writer."

This is news to me. I never read a word Michael wrote. He put out fires. He encouraged me to go to college, but he never went himself. The idea of Michael sitting in Miss Jacks's class, writing haiku, makes something well up in me, and for a minute it's difficult to catch my breath. Even now, after three months have passed, I still have moments where all the air leaves the room for a minute.

"What did . . . did he write?" I have to work to make the words come out.

"Science fiction," she says with a smile. "A couple of westerns. Your brother liked adventure." She makes a small sound, halfway between a laugh and a sigh.

I don't know what to say. I look back and forth between Miss Jacks and the door. Her eyes are misty. "Go on," she says. "Go get the bus."

I don't know her well, haven't done much to draw her attention besides turning in papers and refusing to raise my hand. This is the first time I've really noticed how tired she looks up close.

"Is my—are my poems okay? Do you want me to do them again?"

"They're just fine," she says. "But if you do write more, I'd sure like to read them."

I want to write haiku all the way home, but I can't. Jaina is next to me again and leaves no downtime for thought. She doesn't give me any clues as to why she's trusting me even though I hurt her. She talks about her favorite TV show and her new video game and her upcoming weekend trip to Tennessee. She tells me about the boy she has a crush on and the funny part in the book she's reading and her bad math grade. She tells me she's mad that she has to go straight home today because of makeup work and she can't stay for after-school activities. She barely ever stops for a breath.

"I'm sorry I hit you," I blurt in the middle of her sermon about how unfair Mr. Samples is when he grades his social studies tests.

Jaina laughs this weird little laugh, like a dog barking. "You're a weird kid. You know that, right?"

"Then why'd you sit down next to me?"

"'Cause I'm a weird kid, too. I'm new. All new kids are weird, didn't you know? Least that's what Anthony says." She grins. "I know you was aiming for Anthony, and who can blame you for that?"

"I would like to walk to Town Center."

Phyllis smiles. "A walk sounds nice."

"I would like to walk alone."

Her smile disappears. "I see."

Now I think maybe I hurt her feelings. So I say, "Never mind. Let's stay home."

After Phyllis goes to sleep, I walk to Town Center. It's spooky in the dark. There are ribbons on the trees.

I mean to write. The rules and rhythms of haiku have been bouncing around in my brain since I left Miss Jacks alone at her desk. I have my notebook and my pen and a flashlight I took from the junk drawer in Phyllis's kitchen, and I have all these ideas floating around that are just the right length for haiku. I feel like if I'm going to do them right, I need to be somewhere in nature so I can write about it. I'm not brave enough for the woods at night, so I choose the park.

But in the center of the park, on the steps of the caboose, somebody has placed three hard hats with lamps. One of the hats is red. The ground in front of the caboose is piled with flowers, mostly daisies and baby's breath, along with one carnation—not the evaporated milk but the flower—and a few red roses.

Now there are even more words, too many words for me to write down, bubbling up in my head and through my heart, and I can't make them stop. I hear patterns of syllables in my head, 5–7–5, and they are all about loss and death and sadness and men with grimy faces who leave for work and don't come home. It's like haiku has opened a door inside me that I'm trying with all my might to shove closed again. I feel an itch in my fingers, in my bones. I pull the weeds out of the spaces between the steps of the caboose. I sweep loose twigs off the park bench. I gather the garbage the druggies have left and cram it into the trash can. I try to find the "off" valve for the floodgate of words the sad memorial and my English assignment have opened up.

My fingers twitch toward flowers at the edge of the park. I pick a purple clover and place it on the pile. I do one more haiku in my head:

> If this town were a
> bird, it would not be able
> to fly anymore.

Then I swear off poetry.

11

"I thought you might want to stay for poetry club on Thursdays."

This was not what I expected when Miss Jacks asked me to stay after again. I was thinking maybe she'd had a second look at my poetry and decided it wasn't right after all. My nervousness must show on my face, because she starts trying to talk me into it. "It's Friday now, so you've got almost a week to think about it. Just mull it over, will you? We experiment with new poetry forms. We freewrite. We critique each other's work. A lot of the kids enter contests. There's one every quarter, and they give scholarships."

Scholarships. It's one of those escape words Michael was always pushing me toward, and I latch onto it like a sign from him. Maybe I was too quick to swear off poetry.

"What kinds of scholarships?"

"Well, for talented writers. Some are for specific programs of study, like journalism or English, but a lot of them are just general scholarships."

"How late do you stay?" I ask, wondering how they could squeeze poetry club in before the buses run.

"We meet from three fifteen to four fifteen."

"Oh."

"You would need to arrange a ride home."

"Oh." I leave.

Before the sun rises Saturday morning, I have already worked up a sweat pacing the porch. I've been pacing since Hubert raised one hand in a wave and then walked out to his truck on his first day back at work.

The accident at Dogwood wasn't big enough to close the mine. It was only a little thing, only a fluke. Human error on the part of one of the men who died. It could happen in any job. It's not going to happen again. Everyone is safe; that's what they've said. The mine's open again, barely over a week after the accident.

Still, I pace.

Once the sun is up and the birds are singing right at their loudest, Mikey comes out on his porch. He looks like he just tumbled out of bed: mussed-up hair and sleepy eyes. His glasses are crooked. His shoes are on the wrong feet.

I raise a hand to wave at Mikey like I do to his father.

He waves back. Then he begins pacing his porch and I go back to pacing mine. We haven't stared at each other through the window since we started actually talking, but today there isn't much to say. There's not one speck of humidity, and the porch is warm in the sun and cold in the shade. I stop pacing and sit on the warm part. I worry.

"Can we cook something?" Mikey appears at the porch railing. "I was thinking cake. It doesn't have to be finger-bone cake."

"It's not even nine yet," I tell him. "Phyllis won't let us do cake for breakfast." He looks irritated. "But we can ask Phyllis if we can make more muffins," I offer. "That sounds breakfasty. And then we can put lots of chocolate chips in them."

Phyllis doesn't seem as disapproving of Mikey since he slept on her rug, hugging her dog.

"But we're out of chocolate chips," she says. "If you want chocolate chip muffins, you'll have to go to the store first." She is elbow-deep in a skein of yarn, her knitting needles barely visible. I know there's no chance she'll be going to the store with us. It'll just be me and my cousin. The unexpected freedom sounds like the perfect thing for a Saturday.

"Okay," I say. "We'll go."

"Take some money from the change jar. And ask Shirley first."

We cross to the Harless house to ask Shirley, who's at the computer. Her hair is up under a blue scarf, and the earrings that dangle below it are a matching shade of blue. I think it's funny that she's got her hair put up and her earrings on but she's wearing green plaid pajama pants and flip-flops.

"Can we go to the store?" Mikey asks Shirley.

"I'm busy."

"No, I mean *we*." He points between himself and me.

Shirley turns in her chair, her full attention on us for the first time. She looks from me to Mikey and back to me.

"Can you handle him?" she asks me.

I have no idea, but I nod. "Sure."

"Be back in an hour or I'll worry." Her gaze has already strayed to the screen.

A lot can happen in an hour. But I only say, "All right."

We leave the Harless house and walk through the spring morning with its clean-scrubbed air. Mikey's shoes are still on the wrong feet. I've covered my bare feet with a pair of Phyllis's gardening clogs. We walk up West Lane toward Town Center, Mikey walking slower than I'm used to. I shorten my stride. A few minutes later, I shorten it again. I busy my fidgety feet kicking gravel. It sloshes into puddles of dark yellow mud-water.

"So how come everybody says you're a handful?" I ask him as we pass the caboose and its flowers, which have scattered across the park in the wind.

He shrugs.

"Shirley asked if I can handle you. How come?"

He shrugs.

"I already know you stay up late at night."

"So do you."

"Do you get in trouble at school?"

He shrugs.

"Do you break stuff? Do you run away?" I list my own crimes.

He shrugs.

"You're a man of many words," I comment.

"I want chocolate," he says.

"Where do you think we're going?"

"I'm just saying."

"You're just changing the subject, is what you're doing."

He shrugs.

I point out my apartment as we pass.

"That was mine. Mine with the other Michael Harless."

"The one that died," Mikey says.

I shrug.

The chocolate chip muffins taste even better when we don't put anything but chocolate chips in them. We eat sitting on the porch rail with our feet dangling, watching cars occasionally glide up Route 10. Right in front of Phyllis's porch, there's a pothole. About half the cars swerve and the other half lurch suddenly. When there are no cars, Chip fetches the stick we keep throwing for him. He's a low-slung dog with stubby legs and crooked ears, but he can catch that stick midair almost with his eyes closed.

Every now and then, he lopes toward the road for a drink of water out of the puddle that has formed in the pothole. A group of girls, who walk past in shorts too short for May, look sideways at the dog, like he might bite them. I can catch bits and pieces of their conversation: *"I don't know, what do you think?"* *"It's your hair, Tania."* *"But what do you* think?" Underneath, I can hear the wind gathering and releasing the treetops in the woods behind town. This is the busiest time of day in Caboose.

We throw more sticks for Chip and snack on chocolate chip muffins right down into the evening hours. We don't talk a whole lot. When Mikey talks, it's mostly about gruesome things: how creepy is it that human beings are just skeletons covered in guts covered in skin? And if zombies eat brains, how come they're so dumb? When I talk, Mikey tilts his head at me like he can't work out what language I'm speaking. We don't do well together talking-wise, but we bake three batches of muffins, and by the third, I know how to preheat the oven and grease the pan and even how to use a pot holder safely.

We sit on the porch rail till Hubert comes home from work. His truck grinds into the deeper gravel of the road's shoulder. His door squeaks open. I hurl myself off the porch railing so quick I scratch my knees in the bushes. I dart across both yards to Hubert. I fling my arms around him. Even *I* have not expected me to do this. He almost falls backward and has to steady himself against the truck door. It squeaks again.

"What's that for?" he asks.

"I thought you might die."

He makes a noise somewhere in his throat, like he's got to clear it, and then he tugs me back into a one-armed hug. He smells like dirt and rocks, and I know I'm going to be streaked black when he lets go.

"Jesus, kid," he says, shaking his head, eyebrows disappearing under heavy curls of black hair. "Nah, I'm okay. We're okay."

Mikey sidles up and slips under Hubert's other arm like it's the most natural thing in the world, and the three of us head for the Harless house. For a minute, I feel kinship the way the dictionary defines it, not just shared blood but an actual family. The way I did with Michael and Ben, and maybe even Judy once. Hubert and Mikey are my kin. I still have kin.

"We're okay," I repeat, liking how it sounds.

12

On Sunday it is pouring down sun.
The kind of sun you can't get away from even if you want
to; it's so bright, like orange juice, and it splashes into
everything.

Mikey and I lie on our stomachs on the porch boards
with our chins hanging over the edge. He's drawing in the
dirt with a stick. I'm trying to figure out how to multiply
unlike fractions. Stella's chosen the small of my back as
her perch. She's vibrating her happiness, and I am beginning to get sleepy, even though it isn't even nine a.m.

"We should do something." I feel guilty wasting gallons
of orange sunshine.

"What do you want to do?" Mikey asks.

I shrug half a shoulder. Stella murmurs her disapproval.
"I'm supposed to help your dad clean out the storage
shed."

He snorts. I take this as a no.

"We could go to the pawnshop," I suggest.

"Why? What's at the pawnshop?"

"Something I want."

He twists his head to look over at me. "Something top secret, or you going to tell me?"

"Something top secret."

"You going to tell me when we get there?"

"No."

"Then forget it."

We stay draped on the porch. The sun keeps moving.

"Sasha?"

Mikey's voice catches me off guard. I pull my face off my algebra book, and Stella murmurs another warning.

"I was sleeping," I say.

"Sorry."

"What?"

"I said I'm sorry," he repeats.

"No, I mean, you said 'Sasha.' So I'm saying 'what.'"

"Oh. Let's clean the storage shed."

There's a lot of junk in the storage shed. Some of it is boring stuff: extra extension cords and broken roof shingles and boxes of Christmas lights. Some of it is more interesting. There are stacks of papers arranged loosely on the tops of boxes, like somebody brought them in quickly and stuck them in the first available space, like that person didn't really want to deal with them. They need to be gathered and put into some of the empty boxes along the back.

At first, Mikey stacks things quickly, but after a while, he notices me scanning the papers and separating them into piles to box. Mikey starts scanning, too, like he didn't realize he could do that before.

The top layer of papers is boring. Water bills. Electric bills. Internet bills. Underneath, where the postmarks start getting older, things get more interesting.

After we find the box, Mikey freaks out and breaks a window. I yank him back by the shoulders before he can step on the glass in his flip-flops and get cut. I can't let Mikey step in the glass. He's not even ten. I'm supposed to watch out for him.

Mikey pulls himself from my grip and darts out of the shed. He runs across his yard, across the road, and between two houses on the other side. He disappears from view.

The cousin in me thinks I ought to run after him. But the employee in me thinks I ought to clean up the glass before Hubert sees it, or I might never get Phyllis a GUI-tar.

Actually, the *cousin* in me sort of thinks I ought to clean up the glass before Hubert sees it, too. I can tell Shirley and Mikey barely get along. I want to keep him out of trouble as much as possible.

I'm not exactly sure how to clean up glass. It's scattered all over the rough wood floor of the shed. I know not to pick it up with my hands, but it's going to be tough to clean it up without touching it.

I think I know where Phyllis keeps the broom. It takes some sneaking to get the broom and the dustpan and make it back without anybody asking questions about what I'm doing. Then it takes some figuring to work out how to get the dustpan to hold still while I sweep into it. Nobody ever taught me anything. I feel ashamed and mad all at once. I sweep up the glass, and it makes the softest *crunch-crunch-crunch* as it slides into the dustpan.

Now I've got a dustpan full of broken window and a hand full of broom and a shed that is still not clean and a cousin on the run. The day itself is still pretty, but the stuff inside it isn't.

I hide the broom behind some boxes. I put the dustpan and glass on a shelf. I put the thing away in its box. I close the box. I put it neatly on the shelf in front of the dustpan.

"Sasha?"

Phyllis appears in my doorway. I'm writing haiku. Not for English class but just because. It turns out swearing off poetry doesn't work the way swearing off lima beans does. I swore off lima beans in third grade and it worked. I swore off poetry less than a week ago and here I am.

"Hi, Phyllis."

"Homework?" she asks.

"We learned how to write haiku at school." This is true. It's just not an answer to her question.

"Wow, haiku. I never understood all those forms and patterns. A poem's like kudzu. It's going to grow in the direction it wants. Like a kid."

"I have a poem about plants," I say. I hand it to her. She reads aloud:

> *"Someday I will plant*
> *flowers from West Virginia*
> *in other places."*

She smiles. "That's a good haiku."

"I don't have any haiku about kids."

"That's okay."

"Do you know my English teacher?"

"No, I can't say I do."

"She invited me to poetry club. But I would have to stay after until four fifteen, so I said no."

She makes a mouth noise of disapproval. "Sasha, I can pick you up at four fifteen once in a while. What day is poetry club?"

"Thursday."

"You should have asked me, sweetie."

"I didn't want to interrupt your work."

"Pssh."

We get quiet a minute, but she doesn't leave and she doesn't hum, so I wait.

"Sasha," Phyllis says, "I came up here to ask you a question."

I wait some more.

"Did you break Hubert's shed window?"

I think of how I urged Mikey to help me clean the shed.

"It was an accident," I tell her, which is not a lie.

"Oh, Sasha." She slumps like the air has gone out of her. "Why? Why did you break Hubert's window?"

"There was something in a box," I say.

Phyllis shakes her head. "What box? What do you mean?"

"I wish it didn't happen," I tell her.

She looks so sad that I feel sadder myself. "Sasha, you'll have to pay Hubert for the window," she says, her voice thick with guilt.

I hurt. In my head I hear the final clash of notes the guitar let loose when I threw it against the window.

I pull the suitcase out from under my bed. It doesn't look like a lot of money, the wadded-up bills dried stiff from being damp in my pockets. Phyllis looks from me to the money and back at me with a strange expression.

"Here," I say. "If that's not enough, I'll get more."

Now I'll have to start over. I'm so busy thinking about that, it takes me a minute to realize how much more sad Phyllis looks now that I've given her the money.

13

Phyllis looks and looks for her broom.

Because she doesn't ask me, I never have to lie. She never suspects me. She already caught on that I am the last person to check with for cleaning supplies.

Mikey doesn't come over on Monday. He doesn't come over on Tuesday. By Wednesday, it's warmer than it's been all spring, and Mikey appears next to me.

"Sorry," he says, without saying about what. "I been in trouble for running off."

I'm walking circles in the backyard, letting Chip trail me. I scoot toward the center of the yard so Mikey's got room next to me.

"Me too."

"You're not in trouble no more," Mikey says. "I told my daddy it was me."

I look at him.

"He told Phyllis. And he give back your window money." He talks like his dad. He never says *gave*, always *give*. I like how it sounds, soft like when Hubert described the *fallen-out* between my father's side of the family and his. "I got to pay for it with my next million allowances. I don't think he remembers we haven't done allowance in a year. He brought her broom over, but he couldn't find the dustpan. Why'd you leave the dustpan in the shed?"

I squeeze his hand in thanks. I hear guitar music in my head. I answer his question: "I didn't know what to do with the glass."

Phyllis finds me at four a.m., back in our old spot, sitting on the porch. She's holding a plate of egg salad sandwiches. She must have sensed how I'd be feeling.

"You didn't come to dinner last night," she says.

"I ate," I say quickly, thinking, too late, of how Phyllis was probably worried. Guilt makes me itch. I keep doing things that make Phyllis feel bad. I don't mean to, and I can't always tell that's what I'm doing until it's too late.

"I know you did," she says. "I saw your crumbs on the counter. Didn't think you even liked my corn bread."

"Sorry."

She shakes her head. "No, don't apologize for crumbs, honey. I was just missing you at dinner."

"I figured you had questions."

"I did," she confirms.

"Didn't figure I had answers."

Her mouth tightens, almost like she's keeping in a laugh. She holds out the plate to me, and I take a triangle.

"I get why you took the blame for the window," she says. "You were trying to protect your cousin."

I lean back on the boards, letting my feet hang over the edge of the porch so they can reach the dirt. I eat the egg salad quickly, before it can drip out of the sandwich. A little bit of it falls in my hair.

"The thing is," Phyllis tells me, "if Mikey's breaking windows, he's got some stuff going on. And telling his father, well . . . that lets Hubert help him. So telling the truth is another way of protecting your cousin."

Her logic makes sense, but something still feels wrong, talking about Mikey behind his back. I reach for another half sandwich without sitting up, and she leans down to where I can get to the plate.

"He saw something in a box," I tell Phyllis. "He got so sad."

"I know. Hubert told me a little of . . . well. There's some family business there. He didn't think you'd have Mikey with you when you were working in the shed. And he didn't expect you to open the boxes."

"It fell open." I'm quick to explain away my snooping. "I wasn't going to open it, but it fell."

"Well, shoot. Meant to be, I guess," Phyllis says. "Now the truth is out, Mikey can deal with it."

"He's only little," I say.

"I know." I notice she hasn't eaten a bite.

"There's so *much* sad," I say.

"I know, baby."

With my eyes closed, here in the dark, I'm able to say a little more than usual. "There's my mom and my dad and . . . and Michael . . ." It's still hard to say his name out loud and have him not answer, knowing he'll never answer again. I remember the radio crackling at his funeral, how they called him three times but he never responded. I swallow and keep talking. "And then Mikey's mom and all this new stuff—there's just . . . it's too much, Phyllis!"

"I know, baby," she repeats. She sounds different this time, her voice low and thick.

Right before I fall asleep there on the porch boards, Phyllis says, "I put your money back in your suitcase." There's a silence that sounds like she wants to ask a question, but she doesn't.

I can't find the words to describe how strange it is to see Anthony Tucker in poetry club.

"He always comes," Jaina whispers when she sees me looking. "But if you tell anybody you saw him here, he *will* punch you."

"Naw, I won't, not if you're a girl," Anthony says.

"Yes huh, you told me you'd deck me if I told on you to Will and Jason."

Anthony shoves her playfully with his fingertips. "You ain't no girl!" She makes an ugly face at him and scoots out of his reach, but she doesn't seem truly bothered by his teasing. I don't understand how she's already so friendly with him, and Will and Jason, too. Jaina's new at this school, and she's already making friends. Me, I've gone to school with these people forever, and the only person who's even a little bit like a friend is Jaina.

Miss Jacks is at her desk, juggling two red pens and a highlighter. She misses one and suddenly all three clatter to the desk. Only half the kids spare her a glance, and nobody but me seems surprised at her behavior.

"Sorry," she says when she catches me looking. "I want to learn to juggle. It seems like an important job skill."

I have no idea whether she's joking, so I don't say anything. Miss Jacks retrieves one of her red pens and starts marking things on the paper in front of her. "It's been a long day," she mutters out from under her hair.

"Hey, guys, listen up!" Anthony bosses, as if he's in charge or something. Which, I discover in the next several minutes, he actually is. Anthony Tucker isn't just *in* poetry club. He's the person who started the whole club back in September. "We've got three weeks until the deadline for county, and I want to see at least one entry from every person in this room." He glances at the teacher. "Except Miss Jacks. Because she's old."

"And grading your vocab quiz *right now*, Mr. Tucker . . ."

"And by *old* I mean wise and beautiful," Anthony rushes to add. "For those of you who are new at all this"—he looks at me—"winners of the county contest will go on to the state competition, and the prize at state is a crap-ton of money."

A girl named Lisa who rides the Cary Fork bus raises her hand. Her voice is as proper as her clean polo shirt. I've seen her in the halls, red hair and straight teeth, surrounded by friends. "A five-thousand-dollar scholarship, plus two hundred fifty dollars of spending money."

"Which you won't win if you use words like *crap-ton*," Miss Jacks advises.

"Deadline is the end of June, and the only rules are that it has to be a poem and it has to be written by somebody who, well, you know, goes to school in the county."

A quiet girl in the far corner raises her hand. There is something weird about a kid raising her hand for another kid to call on, but I'm the only one who seems bothered by it.

"Is there a length limit?" she asks. Three or four other kids giggle at her question.

"You always ask if there's a length limit, Angie," says a girl whose name I don't know, "and then you write twenty lines. Exactly twenty lines, every time. So what does it matter, unless the limit is nineteen lines, or it has to be over twenty-one?"

Angie shrugs. "I might do haiku this time, Mel."

"If you do something that short, I'd do three poems," Miss Jacks offers from her spot in the corner. She hasn't looked up from her papers in a while, but at least she hasn't started juggling again, either. "I'd be happy to proofread any entries you feel may need a once-over with a red pen."

"Which is all the entries," Anthony says. "I'm serious, people! Let's not be so last-minute this time, huh? I'm sick of getting our butts kicked at this thing! There's no reason why one of us can't win a stupid scholarship this year. You don't even have to get first place; you just have to be in the top three! Come on, guys!"

"Don't you have to, like, go get up in front of people if you win?" This is one of the few other boys in the room. I can't remember his name, but he's in my math class. He hardly ever says anything out loud.

"I don't know," Anthony says. "You know why? 'Cause we've *never won*."

"We will this year," Miss Jacks says. The conversation has finally pulled her gaze from the papers she's grading. "Right, folks? And yes, Scott, you have to get up in front of people if you win. The winners from every county get to go to a workshop in Charleston, and the top finalists perform their works before the winners are announced. They always have several published authors there to present workshops. It's an amazing opportunity." She looks at Anthony with a raised eyebrow. "Plus, they feed you."

"Why is she looking at *me* on that one?"

"'Cause from what I hear, the entire reason you started poetry club is because Miss Jacks said there'd be food," Jaina points out. "Which reminds me, where's the food?"

Miss Jacks opens her desk drawer and takes out a bag of popcorn. She chucks it into the circle of chairs, where Anthony and Scott fight to gain control of it.

"Guys," Miss Jacks points out, "we're fifteen minutes in, and nobody's learned anything yet. Anybody got some wisdom to impart?"

"I do!" Lisa volunteers. "I'm going to teach you how to write a cinquain. There are a few different types. This one is the kind where the first line is one word, and then you put two words on the second line, three on the third, four on the fourth, and one on the fifth. The first line is a noun, the second is adjectives, the third is verbs, the fourth is emotions, and the fifth one is a synonym for the first one." She beams with self-confidence and eye shadow.

I raise my hand. "Huh?"

"Let me read," Lisa says, a little bit pushy. "You'll hear what I mean. I'll *illustrate* for you what a cinquain sounds like." So I do listen, but I'm flustered because she was so pushy, and I still don't understand the pattern.

"Will you read it again?" I immediately ask.

Lisa fluffs herself and preens. "Of course."
She reads:

> "*Mountains.*
> *Pretty, beautiful.*
> *Rising very high.*
> *Breath taking, awe inspiring.*
> *Appalachia.*"

The group claps, an awkward smattering. Anthony has a coughing fit so long and loud that I worry he's choking on a piece of popcorn.

Lisa reads her poem a third time without being asked.

"*Mountains.* That's my one noun.

Pretty, beautiful. That's my two adjectives.

Rising very high. That's my three words that are a verb.

Breath taking, awe inspiring. That's my four emotion words.

Appalachia. That's my synonym. Because we are *in* the Appalachian Mountains."

Then she claps for herself.

I raise my hand again. "Is *breathtaking* two words?"

"In poetry, you can spell things different," Lisa snaps. "Right, Miss Jacks?"

"Many poets take artistic liberties in their poetry," Miss Jacks allows. When we all keep staring at her, she adds, "Guys, it's after hours. I hope you're not waiting on guidance from me. You all are going to need to keep this rolling without my help. Lisa just taught you how to write a cinquain. Have at it." She waves a hand at the stack of loose paper and the stubs of pencils on the table.

We start shuffling and squinting and doodling. A minute turns into twenty. Cinquain is not as easy as haiku. There are occasional whispers and giggles from the nine kids spread out around the room, and crunching as the popcorn bag gets passed around, and the sounds of scribbling and erasing.

I write:

> Phyllis.
> Pretty, beautiful.
> Patient hands prepare
> four a.m. egg salad.
> Kindness.

I don't show it to anyone, though. I don't know how to explain how four a.m. egg salad is an emotion.

Anthony looks at me for a long minute before sharing his cinquain. I'm pretty sure the look he gives me is meant to communicate how certain my death will be if I ever mention poetry club outside of poetry club. Not that anyone would ever believe me. And who would I tell, anyway, besides Jaina, who's sitting right here? Anthony's got pants that sag to show off his boxers and a plaid button-up over his muscle shirt. He's got a permanent case of hat hair from wearing a beanie at lunch and outside the building and whenever he can get away with it. He does not look "poetry club" to me. If I weren't looking at him right now, I wouldn't believe it.

He reads:

"*Math.*
Topsy-turvy.
Snarling, pencil-tapping.
Paper-ripping frustrated—oh!
Solved."

I can't help myself. "That's good!" I tell him. I'm relieved that cinquains can sound better than Lisa's mountain poem, and surprised through and through that Anthony can write.

"You don't have to tell me." But his grin says he's only teasing. I've never seen Anthony's face look nice before, but right at this moment, it does.

All weekend, I work on cinquains. I start early and work late. By next poetry club, I want to have the perfect cinquain to share with the group. I gaze out the window and off the porch for inspiration. I lie on my back under the trees with their new May leaves in Phyllis's backyard. I wrestle with Chip and Stella when I get bored.

I watch Mikey sit quietly on his porch. I wonder how long his grounding will go on.

I write:

Porch.
Worn boards.
Sit, wait, pace—
lonely, pointless time-wasting.
Creak.

I write:

Caboose.
Too late,
people pile flowers,
sweet and lonely, there.
Heartbreak.

I write:

Box,
secret, dangerous,
taped loosely closed,
falls open and hurts.
Mistake.

I hum my mother's favorite song and I write:

Birds,
feather-quiet,
slice between maples,
calm despite the branches.
Bravery.

Monday, I sneak my cinquains onto Miss Jacks's desk. Thursday is too far away, and the poetry is burning a hole in my pocket.

She sneaks them back onto my desk before the last bell. The bird poem is circled in red.

Oh! she has written in the margin. *Oh, please enter this one, Sasha.*

14

We're sitting at the table, me and Mikey. He is still grounded and is not supposed to be here.

"One of you needs to grease the pan," Phyllis says.

"We do that for pizza, too?" I ask.

"You don't want your pizza to stick any more than you want your muffins to."

Mikey doesn't move, so I grease the pan, since I know how now.

"Mikey, how are you with a can opener?" Phyllis slides him the can of sauce. He tries three times to get the can opener to hook onto the top of the can correctly. He slides the unopened can at me and takes the pan to finish greasing. I open the sauce. Phyllis has put herself in charge of rolling out the dough, since, as she puts it, we are determined not to keep our hands clean. I've been to the sink three times already to wash, at her demand.

"Y'all are some of the gloomiest pizza bakers I ever laid eyes on," Phyllis says to fill the silence.

"I'm sure we'll be more cheerful once the pizza comes out of the oven," I reason.

Once the pizza comes out of the oven, Mikey and I gloomily sit on the front porch, picking off the toppings. Mikey has chosen pepperoni, pepperoni, and more pepperoni, and that seems to be the only part he wants to eat. Mine is mostly cheese with some mushrooms and tomatoes. I eat the mushrooms plain so I can taste them best.

"So what happened?" I ask. I know he knows I'm asking how much trouble he got in for the window.

"I have to see Mr. Powell again. And Shirley, she's real mad. She doesn't like when I act . . ." He wiggles back and forth till he can reach his toes down to the dirt. "She's just mad."

"*My* Mr. Powell?" I've got a mouthful of mushrooms, and I forget to swallow them.

"Gross. Chew your food. I don't know. He's really old and he wears blazers."

"That's *my* Mr. Powell. I didn't know you saw him, too."

He picks at his pepperoni and shrugs with one shoulder.

I make up a cinquain about Mr. Powell and read it aloud:

"Counselor.
Tweed frown.
Always talking down.
Boring, boring, boring, boring.
Cured."

Mikey smiles for maybe the first time since the lid came off the box last week.

Hubert calls me over for a job in the evening. I'm glad, because GUI-tars at the pawnshop have been selling. Two this week. Something about the spring in the air and the warmth of the sun. People want to sit outside and sing so they have an excuse to sit outside or an excuse to sing.

This time Hubert works alongside me. He says it's because it's a big job and he has to do the organizing, but I know it's really because he doesn't want me to read anything else. We go back to the outbuilding, which is still cluttered high with boxes of things. Hubert hands me a trash bag.

"Anything that's wet, toss." I look from the trash bag to the window. It drizzled all night, and dampness has seeped in around the edges of the trash bag Hubert tacked up over the window. The papers we didn't get around to boxing sit in squishy clumps on the shelves.

"Sorry," I say.

"It was my son, not you."

"I was the grown-up," I say, and Hubert smiles a little.

"I'm all the way growed," he confides, "and most of the time I can't tell what Mikey's about to do, either."

"He doesn't mean any . . . he doesn't mean nothing by it."

Hubert takes boxes off a shelf. Without a word, he empties my dustpan of glass into a box and puts the box in the trash bag. He hands me the dustpan.

"He didn't like what he seen," I tell Hubert.

Hubert dusts off the top of a box and moves it to another shelf. "I didn't like what he seen, neither."

Mikey doesn't sleep. He sits at his window and stares at the yard. And I don't sleep. I sit on the opposite side of the glass. Mikey's just a little kid. I don't know how somebody his size could possibly hold all the things I know we're both feeling. I'm afraid if I walk away from the window, when I come back, Mikey won't be there anymore. I don't know where I think he's going to go. I just know that he and I are a lot alike, and that sometimes, when I'm feeling too many things to stand, I run.

When we can't stand sitting still anymore, I take Mikey to Town Center. We sit on a bench. We look at scattered flowers that are getting brown from sun and black from rain.

It's a beautiful night. The only lights are right here

in Town Center, and there are only two of those, one at each end. Still, the sky isn't completely dark. There's enough moonlight to see where the sky ends and the mountains begin. I can hear wind off in the trees, so thick it sounds like running water. I take a deep breath in and smell the wet mud and new leaves of spring.

We don't talk. Mikey and I have a hard enough time talking to each other on a good day. But there are words filling me up, and I need to get rid of them somehow. I sneak loose paper from my backpack. I write:

> Sad things do happen,
> even to little cousins
> who ought to be safe.

I write:

> This town shrinks and shrinks.
> Moms like to sneak out at night
> and never come back.

I write:

> We were all born here,
> but we don't have to die here.
> There is a whole world.

I write:

> I like the wind, though,
> singing like it's been sad, but
> things are better now.

I remember the way I felt the night I swore off poetry—the way the words bubbling up through my heart felt overwhelming, like maybe I could drown in them. Tonight, the words are welcome. I remember being unable to speak after Michael died. I remember not being able to find the words even to describe my own thoughts. It was the reason I kept losing chunks of time and waking up to realize what I'd broken, like the streetlight in Cary Fork, or Phyllis's GUI-tar. Whatever else poetry may do—make me remember, make me think about things—it gives me back the words that I can't always find.

"What did I do?" I ask Mr. Powell the following week. I don't like the sound of a conference, but that's what he's saying we have to have. The more I have to visit Mr. Powell, the more convinced I am that I really do have "friggin' issues." Nobody else in my class sees him, not that I know of. Nobody in poetry club, either. The only other people I know who see him are the kid with no socks and Mikey. And Mikey has "friggin' issues."

"You didn't do anything, Sasha. I'd just like to check in with your foster mother. I haven't met her yet."

"If this is about the rope . . . ," I venture. I figure he must have heard by now that I got in trouble in gym class for scaling a rope and refusing to come down.

Mr. Powell's mustache moves back and forth slightly. "Yes, I did hear about that."

"Miss Jacks says to write, you have to think about perspective. The top of the rope was a different perspective from the bottom. Also, Anthony was at the bottom, and sometimes Anthony . . ."

"Mr. Tucker pushes your buttons."

"Only in the halls. Not . . ." I wonder whether telling Mr. Powell that Anthony goes to poetry club is the same as telling classmates. I decide to be safe and not say anything, which makes two of us; Mr. Powell seems to be waiting for me, and I have no idea what he wants.

"You didn't tell me about poetry club," he prompts at last.

"We learn new forms. There's this contest I might enter. You can win a scholarship."

"That's a great opportunity."

"I wouldn't win. But I might enter."

"Why couldn't you win? Miss Jacks says you're quite talented."

I think about the counselor poem I wrote for Mikey. I

giggle. But this makes me think about Mikey, and I stop smiling. Something about Mikey makes me uneasy lately. Something that feels like worry.

"Sasha?"

I don't care for the way Mr. Powell makes me talk. He asks questions and then he waits and waits to see what spills out. I don't remember what I tell him. Something about cinquains, I guess.

By the time the conference rolls around, I've made myself so nervous about it that I can't even write poetry. This is a problem, since I have a contest to prepare for.

Mr. Powell is always telling me to set goals. Michael always said the same thing. Well, my goal has become winning a poetry scholarship. Since I know now I won't be able to save enough in the suitcase for college—look how long it's taken me just to save half enough for a GUI-tar—I'm going to have to come up with a different plan for leaving.

At the conference, Phyllis smiles and nods and looks serious and is polite. She asks good questions. She doesn't make me feel like I'm in trouble.

At the end of the meeting, Mr. Powell asks me if I'll run an errand for him. I know he can't possibly need twenty-five copies of a leaflet about the PSAT at five in the evening and that he's just trying to get me out of the room, but I like using the copy machine, so I agree.

After I stack the warm copies on top of the machine, I wander around the office. I'm never here after hours, and it's strange to look at the fish swimming in their tank and think about how they live here all the time. One hundred percent of the day, this is where the fish are. They swim in circles. They bump into the little plastic trees and road signs and volcanoes. They eat flakes that you probably don't have to grease the pan to cook. They peek out at kids coming and going, in trouble.

When Phyllis comes out of Mr. Powell's office, she doesn't let me go back in. She tells me we have to hurry if we want to be home in time to fix something hot for dinner. "What did he tell you?" I ask in the car.

"He used a lot of big words," Phyllis says. A few miles later, she adds, "Nothing, Sasha. He didn't tell me nothing."

We roll on for a minute, quiet. Phyllis's car makes soft little rumbles, comfortable like only older engines sound.

"I wish it *was* me that broke the window," I say.

"Mr. Powell mentioned that," she tells me. I'm surprised. I don't remember intending to tell Mr. Powell about that. It must have slipped loose when I was thinking about Mikey.

"Why do you wish that?" Phyllis asks. She doesn't sound like she's judging, only curious.

"Because Mikey's only little," I say. "He should get to be normal and grow up normal and go to college."

Phyllis laughs. "I don't know if you've been to a college,

girlie, but it ain't exactly teeming with normal people."
She laughs again. "Never mind. Mikey'll be fine, Sash.
He'll get to go to college, and so will you, if that's what
you want."

"It is." I feel like my brother is sitting right next to me.
I can almost smell him, a mix of sweat and smoke and
cologne. "I want me and Mikey both to get to leave." For
reasons I don't completely understand, it's becoming important to me that if I get out, Mikey does, too.

"Hmm."

We drive on in silence for a minute before I think to
ask, "Why did you never leave?"

She glances at me. "Caboose?"

"Yeah."

"What makes you think I never left?"

My head whips around. "You did?"

"On my nineteenth birthday. Me and Heath Christian
drove for days. We took turns sleeping in the passenger
seat. We got lost probably half a dozen times and kept
ending up in weird parts of Ohio, but we finally got going.
When we were both awake, we couldn't stop pointing out
all the things was different over that way."

"Which way was that?"

"We drove west. We were hell-bent on California, but
long about western Missouri, the weather started looking
a lot nicer outside the car than in it. He found a job doing

truck maintenance for a big rig outfit, and I found out I was expecting Miles."

I watch the headlights reflect off the white line that disappears and reappears along the crumbling edge of the road. "Why'd you come back?"

"Heath Christian didn't turn out to be quite the man I thought he was," she said, "and I found out I was expecting Sam. I needed help, and my family was here."

"Do you still have family here?"

"Sure I do," she says. "An aunt and a cousin. Mostly the others are with your brother, but they're still *here*. I can visit them up on the mountain. I can feel their presence." She readjusts her grip on the steering wheel and makes a couple of small noises before she finds any more words. "This is where I choose to be, Sasha. My people are here."

I try to imagine how it feels to *choose* Caboose. As long as I can remember, I've never considered that it was a choice. Michael wanted to escape so badly that his plan always felt like my own. Even now, as comfortable as I've started to feel with Phyllis, something in me still burns to escape. Sometimes, when I get frustrated at school or scared about things, I imagine running away again. I could take the money in the suitcase and use it to buy nice clothes that make me look older. I could get a job—maybe not something official, maybe just odd jobs like I'm do-ing now, but it would be enough to buy food, enough to survive until I'm grown and can get one of those scholar-ships or college loans that Michael was always shoving me toward.

My plan isn't that simple anymore. I still want to follow Michael's wishes and leave the state. But now I'd want to take Mikey with me. He's a Michael Harless, too, even if he has another name before it. He's like another chance for Michael to get away. He should grow up someplace without secret papers in boxes. He should grow up some-place safe.

"If I left, I'd miss your songs," I blurt out. I glance side-ways at Phyllis. "And egg salad."

"I'd like it if you didn't leave again," Phyllis says. "I've chased you down enough, sweet girl."

"I know it. I didn't mean now. I mean later. When I'm grown." It's only a partway lie.

"Later, when you're grown," she tells me, "you can choose a place to live that feels right to you. But it has to feel right to *you*, Sasha. Not to me or Mr. Powell or your brother, or to anybody else."

I am all full up with choices. I lay my head on the window, overwhelmed, and fall asleep before we reach Caboose.

15

It's Thursday, which means poetry club, and I've been looking forward to it all day long. The buses pull away past the windows while kids bang locker doors closed out in the hallway. Poetry club kids come in one or two at a time, snagging popcorn or pushing chairs together to sprawl out on, until there are nine of us in the room, plus Miss Jacks.

I love how different the classroom is now from how it was twenty minutes ago in English class. It doesn't feel formal anymore. Kids make themselves at home, getting comfortable. I'm surprised how quick they've accepted me as one of the group. They've accepted Jaina, too, even quicker than me. She acts like she was born here. The two of us sit on the floor side by side. Jaina's tossing a beanbag back and forth with Angie, who suddenly wings it at

Anthony's head. He catches it almost without looking, and Jaina applauds.

"Who wants to start?" Anthony asks, tossing the bean-bag into the air and catching it a few times. "Oh, wait, wait, that'd be *me*. I need everybody to write down their email addresses if I don't already have them. That means you"—he points at Jaina—"and you." He points at me. "I'm going to email you the contest rules, and I want everybody to email me back a poem. *Everybody!* Email me back a poem by this time next week! The deadline's at the end of the month, and the next one's not till August! I need your entries so I have time to let Miss Jacks tear them to pieces!"

"Give constructive feedback," Miss Jacks corrects.

Anthony rips a sheet of paper from his notebook, tears it in half, and paper-airplanes each half to me and Jaina. "Writing down your email address means I have express permission to email you the summer newsletter."

"Is there poetry club in the summer?" Jaina asks.

"No, but like I said, there's a newsletter. And that news-letter, penned by author, poet, and world-class journalist Anthony Tucker"—he takes a bow—"will suggest various poetry forms you can be practicing so that when we come back at the end of August, you'll have something written for the competition. Because, so help me, people, some-body who is sitting in this room right now had better win one of those scholarships—*or else!*"

I'm not wild about the idea of Anthony Tucker having my email address. I write it down, but I don't hand it back yet.

"Now. Who wants to start?"

"I wrote an acrostic," Lisa volunteers, puffed up with importance.

Anthony chucks the beanbag at her and she jumps, startled, and misses it. Angie kicks it back over to her, and she picks it up by a corner. "What do I do with this?"

"It means you have the floor," Anthony says. "Take it quick, before I change my mind."

"Like you can stop me from talking."

"Go on, go on. An acrostic?"

"I remembered it from elementary school, and I looked it up online. It's where you use the letters of a word, like your name, as the first letter in each line. Like—okay, I'm Lisa. So I wrote *L–I–S–A* down the page, and each of those letters is the first letter in that line."

She reads:

> *"Little girl*
> *Is growing up*
> *So fast.*
> *Almost adult."*

I actually like this, but I can't bring myself to tell Lisa. Something about her polo shirt and her thin, straight, neatly cut red hair. If I think it's hard talking to Jaina, I'd probably never manage to pull together any words to say to Lisa. I can't imagine we have much in common.

"Can we do other people's names?" Anthony asks, super casual. His eyes also stray to Lisa. I work to hide a giggle.

I see Miss Jacks fight a smile before she says, "Let's stick to our own names for the moment. It's much safer."

We take a few minutes to write. But I don't like this form. It sticks to my pencil.

Still, it's kind of cool how many directions the members of poetry club take with each letter. In different kids' poems, the letter C might stand for *Cheetos*, *Camping*, or *Courageous*.

When Anthony tosses me the beanbag, I read:

"So
Annalisa
Suggested we all use our
Heads and write
Acrostic poems. Ugh."

Lisa shrieks with displeasure. "My name isn't Annalisa. It's just Lisa!"

"Well, that would make my name S-*llll*-sha! And you don't have the beanbag!" Turns out she's not so hard to talk to after all, once she's got me mad.

"Girls," Miss Jacks interrupts before me and Lisa can come to blows over who gets to keep her given name. "Consider it artistic license," she tells Lisa. Then to me: "Consider putting your shoulder into the assignment."

So I write:

> Someday I will
> Answer when
> Somebody asks me a question I wish they
> Hadn't
> Asked.

I look up to find that Lisa has been reading over my shoulder. Rage burns.

"You don't read over a person's shoulder; that's . . . that's rude!" The words will hardly spit out. I see the other kids look up.

"You don't have the beanbag!" Lisa mimics. "Anyway, that doesn't make any sense! That's not a poem about you, just because it has your name in it."

"How about we keep the tempers in check?" Miss Jacks suggests.

"It says *Sasha*, doesn't it?" I snap. "So shut up. What did you write?"

"I already did mine!"

"Girls." Miss Jacks is standing now.

"Okay," me and Lisa both mutter. I scoot even farther away.

There is silence for a minute. Then Jaina raises her hand and Angie tosses her the beanbag.

Jaina reads:

"Joyful
And
Interesting.
Never forget to be
Awesome."

"That's not about you, either," Lisa mutters, but Miss Jacks silences her with a raised eyebrow.

"I like it," I say, a little louder than necessary, because I want my voice to matter more than Lisa's. Anger has made me less shy and given me a little more volume.

Jaina watches me long past her turn. When I catch her eye, she glances toward Lisa and then, when she is very sure Lisa isn't looking, sticks out her tongue. Some of the tension bleeds out of me, and I smile back, glad I haven't scared Jaina off with my temper.

Anthony raises his hands for the beanbag, and a smile creeps onto my face before he can even start reading. I'm surprised to find how much I'm looking forward to his words.

He reads:

"Anthony is
Never on
Time for anything, Mrs. Tucker.
He needs to turn in his homework
Or he will flunk.
Next week is report cards.
Yes, that's right. Next week."

Everybody laughs. But I notice Anthony doesn't laugh much. Miss Jacks was wrong. Writing about our own names isn't safe at all.

I look at Anthony, but he never looks back. He's missed a few opportunities to pick on me since last poetry club. It's almost like we're friends now because we share Thursdays.

So I write:

Anthony is
Never as boring as
The other kids.
He writes
Okay poetry and
Never forgets to be funny.
Yes, that's right. Funny.

I don't read it out loud, because it has broken the rule about other people's names. When we're leaving, I want to hand it to Anthony, but I'm too shy. *Maybe next time*, I think. For now, I keep it in my notebook, and I hand him my email address instead.

Phyllis drives slowly through the rain. I gaze out the window at wet springtime leaves. Dead leaves from last fall still coat the ground. They're grimy from passing trucks. I reach across the front seat and take Phyllis's hand. She squeezes my fingertips with hers.

16

"Sasha, hold it still. Don't move it so much." I've never heard Phyllis's voice sound quite so high-pitched. It's still Thursday, but much later, and Phyllis is reaching across the car, holding Shirley's dish towel against my hand.

"You're squeezing too hard!" My voice sounds strange. Too slow or something.

"I have to squeeze," Phyllis says. "I have to stop the bleeding. I know it hurts—"

"No, it doesn't." It really doesn't. I wonder if that's a good thing or a bad thing.

After poetry club, we'd gone home as usual. Phyllis started dinner, and afterward, we made dessert. We were going to take some to Mikey and the girls, but we only got halfway through the yard to their front porch before we heard Shirley screaming.

I ran ahead, ignoring Phyllis's hollering for me to stop, and I found Mikey crouched in a corner of the kitchen with his hands over his head while Shirley hit him with the dish towel.

It was only a dish towel and it couldn't really hurt him, but the anger pouring out of Shirley made me feel cold and hot all at the same time, and she kept hitting and hitting him, and he wasn't doing anything besides sitting there. In another corner of the kitchen, Sara and Marla sat on the floor, both wailing. Marla's high chair was turned over, and Sara had her sister on her lap, their arms and legs all tangled up.

I hollered for Shirley to stop, and when she didn't, I wrenched my sleeve from Phyllis's grip and went in swinging. Shirley ducked, but her kitchen window didn't. Maybe I hit it at just the right angle, or maybe it was weak from all the hot dishwater she was always running below it. Whatever the reason, it shattered before I even understood what was happening.

Shirley followed us out of the house. She'd always been so grim and quiet, it was a shock to see her screaming and sobbing. Phyllis held a dish towel, the same one Shirley'd been swinging, around my bleeding hand. She was maneuvering me and Mikey both out of the house when Shirley grabbed a handful of Phyllis's jacket.

"He knocked the baby out of her high chair."

At that, Phyllis stopped, a shudder going through her

like she just plain couldn't figure out how she was going to manage one more child with her current number of hands. "Is the baby all right?"

"No thanks to him!" Shirley was coming unglued completely. Her voice was pitched shrill and she didn't seem to know what to do with her hands. They fluttered around her throat, then stretched out toward us through the air. I could see them shaking. I wondered if she would remember this later, because I recognized in her the same out-of-control that I'd been more than once, and I didn't always remember everything later.

"I didn't mean to!" Mikey hiccupped. "I was . . . I was just running—I didn't want the TV—" He stopped. "Dad didn't come home!"

"There's been another one," Shirley said at last, something about her voice making all of us feel cold.

There's a doctor stitching my hand, so I can't write. I have to do it in my head.

I think:

> *Something bad happened*
> *at the Dogwood Number Six.*
> *Hubert's not home yet.*

But this doesn't explain what really happened, so I write:

Fire
and smoke
block rescuers from
telling us the truth
tonight.

But I haven't followed the rules, and this is not a true cinquain.

So I write:

Mikey got upset.
He tried to run, didn't mean
to hurt the baby.

But this doesn't explain that the baby fell. That Mikey knocked her out of her high chair. He wasn't trying to hurt Marla. He was trying to run from the house before the TV man could say what happened.

So I write:

Shirley lost her head.
She's worried about Hubert.
I guess she loves him.

I wish I knew what to say to Mikey. He's sitting in the corner of the exam room with his knees pulled up to his chest, looking small, small, small.

· · ·

In the dark night, Mikey's house is lit. Nobody's been to bed. The same lights are on as when we left. Shirley's pacing, holding Marla, who is screaming, red-faced, and trying to get down. Shirley doesn't seem to notice, but she's patting the baby's back with each step. Sara's on the porch boards, wearing only a diaper, running a three-legged toy horse back and forth. She makes it jump the cracks.

Hubert might not come back.

The thought steals my breath. Hubert's scrub-brush beard and his crinkled, kind eyes might be gone forever from my life and from Mikey's. I don't want Mikey to hear the news. I don't want *me* to hear the news. After the call comes, everything will be different. Everything will be darker. I've waited for this sort of news before. Sometimes it seems like I'll always be waiting for phone calls in the dark.

Mikey stays over. Nobody suggests that he go inside with Shirley. He doesn't talk to me and Phyllis about what happened. We wait, but the headlights never arc across my window like they do when Hubert comes in after dark. We don't admit we're waiting. We just keep staring at the window.

Phyllis and I sing to Mikey. He's outgrown songs at bedtime, but he tolerates us with a tired smile too old for nine. We work our way through all of Phyllis's standby favorites: Joan Baez, Bob Dylan, a Beatles song or two. Then all her old folk songs. So many of them are sad. She stops halfway through my mother's song, like she's just realized it's the same one that led me to break her guitar. But I meet her eyes and keep singing. It seems so long ago, that day I broke the guitar. It was only three months ago, only three months since I moved into Phyllis's house, but in the days since, there's been Mikey and there's been Phyllis and there's been poetry club, and everything's been better.

It was a trick; it was all a trick. I can see it now. I started to relax and then something awful happened. I understand my mother's song now. When Phyllis pauses, I keep singing "A Bird in a Gilded Cage," and after a few lines, she joins me again. It's all about being trapped and unhappy, and the only way out is to die. That must have been how my mother felt, trapped in a place where nothing ever really changes.

I hold Mikey tight as we sing. That will not be our escape. Not like Ben and Michael and maybe Hubert. I'll make sure we have a chance to grow up outside this cage. I won't get tricked again into staying.

We fall asleep after three and get woken up by the ringing, like the sound in your ears after you fall. The lights are still on, and we are all propped on the same bed like throw pillows. When Phyllis leaves to answer the phone, the room starts to seem smaller, the walls close, the lights dim. Mikey looks at me and doesn't speak. It seems stupid of us to just sit here and wait.

As dawn breaks, before Phyllis has a chance to come and tell us the news, I take Mikey and we leave this place.

part two

17

Yesterday was late May, and today is late May, but the difference between yesterday and today is the difference between a blizzard and a summer-day picnic. The whole heavy world is pressing down on us, and Mikey keeps stumbling. I pull him up by his arm over and over again. I won't let him fall.

It takes half a day in the woods to realize I'm completely useless. I've never learned how to hunt, fish, gather, scavenge, keep myself alive off the land. I've never learned how to hike, navigate, trailblaze. No one ever taught me how to scale a rock cliff or comfort a child. I don't know the first thing about making clothing out of plant fibers.

Mikey rips his jeans in two places in the first hour.

He had a run-in with a creek bed. He's wet and muddy. His underwear is showing. I didn't think to pack us clothing. I brought the suitcase with the money, but I didn't think to put clothing in it. I've packed an empty suitcase.

We drink from the creek, which tastes like coal smells. I remember that we have to drink, or when they catch us, they'll send us to the hospital. I can feel the stitches making my right hand itch, and I'd just as soon not go back to the hospital again.

I'm not Phyllis—I can't manage singing at a time like this. But I think Mikey needs to hear my voice. I guess I know that the same way Phyllis always knows when I need egg salad at four a.m. So I recite poetry while we walk. I tell him Anthony's best poems. I tell him Lisa's bad poetry, which would make him giggle if he wasn't crying. I tell him my Mr. Powell poems and my Michael and Ben and Judy poems and my bird poems. I tell him new poems I make up about the brambles and the coal creek and the walking.

> "Coal,
> black, invisible,
> lives all over.
> Can't get away from
> it."

And:

"Here in the black creek,
water comes and water goes.
So do you and I."

And:

"Walking.
Slow steps.
Picking through brambles.
Someday we'll get there.
Wherever."

We eat a million skimpy strawberries. Mikey doesn't speak all morning, and I keep telling poetry, keep praying poetry.

It was Michael's job to make the escape plan, and he did, but now he's gone and his plan won't work because it involved a car and grown-ups and college scholarships. So now it's my job to make the plan. If we follow the creek, we'll hit Route 10 between Bent Tree and Dower's Fork. From there, we can quit following the creek, with its briar bushes and mosquitos, and start following the road. The road will take us out of the county, and that, for the moment, is enough of a plan. We aren't so much going *to* somewhere as we are coming *from* somewhere. Behind us are sad things. Boxes in sheds and phones that ring in the

157

night. Fires that take away brothers and coal mines that take away fathers and mothers that go away. Up ahead are the things Michael promised. A different sort of life.

At first, I miss Phyllis terribly. I pick at the bandage on my hand. I think about how she sang for me while the stitches went in. I'm ashamed to have left without buying her a GUI-tar. But after night has come and gone, after we've walked till I can't think of anything but walking, thoughts of Phyllis and of Hubert—thoughts of all of Caboose—are like the flowers in Town Center that blew away. All that remains is a faint scent, like rotting fruit, and a memory too vague to pick out specific kinds of flowers. All you know is there were petals. All you know is you have left them.

Following a creek through the woods on a West Virginia mountain is easier said than done. Our creeks aren't polite. They spill sideways down rock cliffs. They churn and worry. They wear a path through solid rock.

And our foliage. Isn't that what people call it? I call it brambles. I call it briars. We're both scratched and sweaty. Mikey winds ahead of me, and branches slap backward to hit me in the face. I've been out of breath all day.

Phyllis—who has become one of the voices in my head—says I should think positive. And I do. I'm positive I am about to die of a heart attack. I've spent three months lying on my back on worn porch boards. I'm not in shape for hiking.

There are words and phrases stuck in my head. Now that I've been reciting poetry, the floodgates in my brain are open and words are filling me up. Words like *escape* and *flee* and *run*.

Mikey complains that he is too tired to go on.

I've got to get us to the road.

18

The creek takes us to the bridge and the bridge takes us to the highway and the highway takes us to the town of Dower's Fork, where I stop at Gas-Quik and fill the suitcase with bread and peanut butter, crackers and cakes. I remember to buy bottles of water that won't taste like coal. Now the suitcase is heavy.

My original plan was only to get us out of Caboose, and here we are in Dower's Fork, someplace new. But Dower's Fork feels the same as Caboose, gray and gritty. I want us to end up someplace clean and fresh, someplace that doesn't smell like coal or floodwaters, someplace where the headlines aren't so sad. I'm not completely crazy. I know it won't be easy, just the two of us kids on our own. But we're strong, me and Mikey. We can make it work. We can find someplace dry and warm to stay, and I can do odd jobs for other people instead of Hubert. I can save money and we can buy clean clothes that make us look older, and we can enroll in school again and study hard until it's time for college.

Me and Mikey both will be going to college. I've decided. It's what Michael always wanted for me, and as for Mikey, well . . . I'm not going to let another Michael Harless miss out on seeing the world.

The sides of the highway are chipping. The pavement is cracking. We keep our heads down. We catch ourselves trying not to step on the cracks.

Mikey doesn't speak, and I've run out of poetry. I'm trying to make up new poems, but I can't remember the forms. Poetry club is at school. We're walking in the other direction. I'm out of range of poetry club.

I think of hitchhikers. I think of those people in movies who hop into train cars. I think of how hot-wiring might work. I study the tired horses we pass in a crooked pasture by the road.

I'm not as brave as I want to be. We walk.

It's night. The kind with no stars. Then it's morning. The kind with red sunrise.

Dawn and the thunderstorm break at around the same time. Mikey's broken, too. He's sniffling. Tears drip off the end of his pointy chin. His lip juts out like a much smaller child's, and I wish I wasn't too tired to scoop him up to carry. He's scared. He's tired. He wants his daddy. He wants to go home.

I can't let us turn around. I can't let us give in to being tired and scared. There's nothing left behind us but bad news.

I tell him, "I know there's a home for us up ahead." I know he knows I'm lying, but neither of us says it.

He doesn't want to walk, so I pull him. I feed him peanut butter and pour the water into him. I feed him dusty strawberries growing too close to the road. A field opens up beyond the berries, and I know we've made tracks. There are no open fields down our way. There are only steep cliffs and filthy trees and twisting roads.

I tell him, "We're almost there." He doesn't ask where. I don't tell him what I know: we're in the middle of nowhere. Wherever *there* is, we won't see it for days. This is maybe the stupidest thing I've ever done. But my feet refuse to turn us around. *We can't go back. We can't go back.*

Mikey is stained pink from the strawberries. His tears make clean tracks through all the pink.

We fall asleep under the raindrops, out in the open. The grass makes us itch. It's dusk. The sky leans low. Mikey cuddles up to me. He holds my arm like a teddy bear. He's so little, here in the grass. I pet his hair like he's a kitten, and he doesn't shake me off.

I tell him, "We have to be there, almost."

I tell him, "Hang on another day."

Every once in a while, I'm overwhelmed by images of Hubert fixing the porch rail or holding one of the babies or looking lovingly at Mikey without realizing he's doing it. I feel an ache welling up that only walking will numb.

I tell Mikey, "We have to hang on another day."

We hang on another day, and it's dry. The sun comes out. We're tired beyond tired. We're filthy beyond filthy. We are not just walking. We have *become* walking. There's nowhere we are going. But it's good. There's nowhere we're coming from. We are simply steps. *Step. Step. Step.*

Stepping is getting easier because, away from home, the land gets less steep. The mountains become hills. The hills are dotted with pretty things. Wild carrots. Mayapple. Pale yellow coltsfoot. Not the part of a horse, but the plant. The trees are pretty here, too. They're not gray. They're greener than green.

Morning fades like blue jeans, and the midday sky is pale. Clouds wisp by. Mikey isn't crying. He breaks the tops off weeds as we walk. He kicks gravel into the road.

Midday deepens like water, and the evening sky is beautiful. The blue is *so* blue. The sunlight is orange and thin. We're walking in a high meadow, grass and flowers all around us. Off to the left are flat-topped mountains with no trees—a strip mine. Ben used to talk about working the strip job, blasting off the tops of mountains to get at the coal underneath. The field we're walking in might have been a strip mine once, but there are flowers now and open spaces, and the openness makes me feel like I can get a breath for the first time in days.

Down below us, where the land drops off at the end of the meadow, the trees spring up like a boundary fence and then thin out. The fields give way. There are power poles. There are streetlights blinking on. We've made it to a new place.

My feet slow, then stop altogether. Mikey walks six or eight more steps before he, too, grinds to a halt, blinking at me as if waking from a dream.

"We did it," I tell him. It's the first word either of us has spoken since yesterday.

"Did what?" His voice sounds scratchy and tired, but familiar and welcome under the blanket of summer bugs and treetop wind.

"We . . . we got here."

"Where?"

I'm so tired, I'm confused by his question. "Well . . . well, how should I know? Let's go see."

The sign says ALLEY RUSH. It's surprising to end up some-place I already know. I've been through it a few times. It's a town beside a town. If you keep going, you get to bigger places. You get to Hart with all its houses. Way on up, you get to Beckley with its mall. You get to the interstate that

takes you to Charleston, and from there you can get anywhere, because Charleston is near everything.

"We walked six hundred years to get to a place we
coulda drove in a half hour?" Mikey asks. He seems less
than impressed with my running-away skills, but I'm too
distracted to care. I'm so relieved that it makes me shake.
We aren't wandering in the wilderness anymore. I haven't
lost us; I haven't gotten us killed out in the woods. Then,
quick as the relief came, terror sets in. We're near places
now, and I'm not interested in being near anything. I don't
want to get found.

But Alley Rush is small. Maybe it's okay to stop here for
a while. There are flowers springing up along the streets,
so precise I know they were planted. Tame wildflowers—
tameflowers?—in groups by color. I don't see mayapple or
wild carrots or coltsfoot. I don't see anything here that I
saw in the woods.

Mikey says, "Dang."

He's looking at a street vendor opening his stand. The
vendor cranks down one cloth sign at a time: HOT DOGS.
CHEESEBURGERS. CHOCOLATE-DIPPED FRUIT.

"Dang," I echo.

There is a banner above the city:

121ST ALLEY RUSH HARDWOOD FESTIVAL

CARNIVAL! GAMES! PARADE! SHOPPING!

"We're just in time," I say.

"Caboose has its carnival in a couple weeks," Mikey said. "I mean, if you were gonna walk that far for a carnival."

"Mikey—"

"I'm just saying."

"We didn't walk to the carnival. We walked to . . . we walked to *get somewhere*."

He shakes his head at the sky as if asking God for patience. It's one of the mannerisms Mikey learned from Hubert, and it makes my muscles all go tense at the same time. Now that we're not walking, the loss of my cousin might catch up. I can't let it.

"Hey, did I ever tell you about the time my brother and I walked for twenty-four hours straight, just to see if we could?"

"No . . . ," Mikey says. "You didn't tell me that one. But that would have been good to know *before* I walked off into the woods with you. Might have give me some clue we were going to walk for*ever*."

"Just to see if we could," I repeated. It's only partway true. Me and Michael walked just to see if we could, but we also walked to see if things felt different when we got back. It was only a week after Ben died, and when we got back, Michael got practical. He started working at the grocery store and quizzing me on spelling words. He started making plans for us to leave.

The street vendors won't open their stands until it gets all the way dark. Our stomachs growl at sights and smells. We sit on the curb. Mikey stretches his legs out in front of him and leans back on his elbows. For a moment I'm struck by how much like my brother he looks, all casual.

"Well?" he asks. "Could you?"

"Huh?"

He rolls his eyes. "Walk for twenty-four hours."

"Give or take." We were gone a day and part of a night. I don't fill him in on the hours spent sitting with our backs against trees while one or the other of us cried.

"Opening-night special," a man in a hat calls into the growing crowd. "Two footlongs, two dollars! Opening-night special, people! Get your footlongs!"

My hand uncurls from the suitcase. My fingers are cold from being wet. I scratch and scramble at the clasps until the case comes open. I snatch out two dollars, a third for tax, in case they charge it. I slam the case shut before anyone can see I'm carrying money. My brother taught me to always keep it hidden.

I catch up to the hot dog man and shove two dollars into his hand. "One with everything"—I don't know what *everything* is, but the more food, the better, I figure—"and one with ketchup." Because I know Mikey won't eat whatever *everything* is.

The man's gaze slides from the dollars to my filthy hand. To my filthy face. To my filthy cousin.

"Y'all been enjoying the festivities already," he comments. He takes the dollars, no tax, and serves up the hot dogs. He keeps looking. I take Mikey by the elbow and thread us back into the crowd.

Everything turns out to include at least two things I don't recognize. Still, food is food, and I don't much care what it tastes like. We eat while we watch the narrow streets of Alley Rush fill up with people. Some of the people are dressed the way they would have been at the very first Alley Rush festival, in gingham and in overalls, as if they've come in from the farm. I know they're dressed this way only for today, because their clothes are clean, and because this isn't how farmers dress anymore. I see real farmers in town sometimes. They wear tan work boots and T-shirts with rectangles worn in the pockets from their cigarette packs.

Every power pole in Alley Rush has got a yellow ribbon tied around it. At first I wonder why, and then I feel stupid for wondering why. Just because I haven't been watching the news doesn't mean every other person in the region hasn't. The fact that the signs and ribbons are up tells me everything I need to know: the accident at the mine was bad. The ringing phone Phyllis went to answer would have brought us terrible news.

All the church signs have had the letters rearranged till they say something about the miners from down our way: GOD BLESS OUR MINERS and WE LOVE OUR MINERS and PRAYERS WITH THE FAMILYS, which is spelled wrong, which makes me feel like crying. I know there isn't a city in the region that doesn't have the fate of the Dogwood miners in mind. It doesn't matter whether the town's got mines of its own. We all feel it when something bad like this happens.

There are booths all up and down the street. Nearly every one has a sign announcing it sells something carved out of certified Alley Rush hardwood. There are game booths for knocking over bowling pins carved out of hard-wood. There are antique booths stocked with old figurines carved out of hardwood. I look around. Alley Rush was carved out of hardwood. The only trees still growing in city limits are saplings, young and skinny like Mikey.

There's a live band, too. They're not very good, but no one seems to care. People are dancing in the street. The later it gets, the more people dance, and the fewer of them are kids. If this were a movie town, there would be a clock in the square. I duck to look at a man's watch as he reaches for a footlong. It's nearly midnight.

It feels so good to be full. It feels so good not to be walk-ing. I feel so good, I sweep Mikey into the street. We spin. We dance. It feels good to dance. Lights spin around us.

We spin around each other. Our feet get faster the more tired we get. We sing songs we don't know the words to. We hold on to each other's hands so tight we might never be able to let go. We laugh like happy people. We breathe air that's getting colder.

Later, we stop dancing, but the world does not stop spinning. We lie down on the grass of someone's lawn. The world still does not stop spinning.

19

A voice comes out of the dark.

"Why we doing this, Sasha?"

There is faraway laughter and the shouts of drunk people as the town slowly comes down from its Hardwood Festival high. The grass under my head is dry. No dew means it's going to rain soon. I hope not tonight. A better guardian would find shelter for Mikey, but I can't get up off this grass. I can hear dogs barking and, in the distance, the Jake brakes of some truck heading away down Route 10. Those sounds are familiar, but there are fewer birds and bugs singing here in the darkness than there are back home. I guess that makes sense, if there are fewer trees.

It's hard to find the right words in the right order, but I can hear from Mikey's breathing that he's still awake and waiting. Somewhere in me, the poetry flickers to life again and gets my words unstuck.

I say:

> *"Outside of Caboose,*
> *people laugh more than they cry,*
> *and we deserve that."*

There's a long quiet, so long I think Mikey's gone to sleep there in the dark beside me. But then the tired little voice finds me again. "That's bull," he says. "I laugh plenty back home."

> *"Whenever we laugh*
> *back home, we know there's a chance*
> *bad news is coming."*

It doesn't sound like a poem, but I like picturing the line breaks in my head.

"Sasha?" The pause is longer this time, and his voice is smaller. I abandon the poetry now that it's gotten me started.

"Yeah, Mikey?"

"Is my dad dead?"

I'm glad it's dark so my cousin can't see the tears that start to roll out of the corners of my eyes, down the sides of my head, and into my hair. I wipe my nose on my sleeve instead of sniffling out loud. I don't want Mikey to hear me.

"Is he?" Mikey asks again.

"The longer we're gone," I say, "the longer we don't have to know. And the longer it'll be before anybody else goes away."

There's quiet while he mulls. I know he's mulling and not sleeping because he makes little thoughtful noises and hauls in shaky little breaths.

"Okay," he says finally. Lying wide-awake in the grass in a strange town, watching black clouds turn silver in front of the moon, he agrees to my plan. "Okay. We can run away."

"I'm glad you think so, since we already did."

20

I wake already knowing things have changed.

Mikey is tugging on me. Pulling on my sleeves. His voice slides in from somewhere else. I think I might be underwater.

"Wake up, Sasha! C'mon, wake up!"

I do, at last. I sit, and the world is *still* spinning. It's full, bright daylight, and Mikey and I are no longer alone.

"Young lady," says the police officer in his uniform, which, up close, is not as crisp as I would have thought a policeman's uniform would be. His face is marked with stubble, as though policing the festival has worn him out. "Are you all right?"

"Oh." I get to my feet, but it takes me a minute to remember we're in Alley Rush. The festival is getting under way again. The sidewalks are full of clumps of kids walking together, teenagers in school shirts, laughing.

"Young lady?"

"Oh." I focus on the officer. "Oh. I'm fine. Yes, sir, thank you. I'm fine."

But he's not satisfied. He waits.

"We stayed out late last night at the festival. I guess I fell asleep." I sound more normal than normal. I sound more normal than Lisa.

He keeps looking. I start to hustle Mikey away. The officer puts out a hand to stop us.

"Young lady, I need you to stay with me for a moment." He's reaching for something. A gun, maybe. Worse. A radio.

The radio makes something inside me shake. As it crackles, I remember the final call for Michael at his funeral. I remember how the air went quiet when he didn't answer. He's buried now in Caboose, and he'll be there forever; he'll never get out.

If this police officer takes me and Mikey back, we might never get out, either. This is it—our now or never.

I tug on Mikey and he follows me, too slowly. I shove him ahead of me, hard. *This* Michael Harless will get away. I'll make sure of it.

We make it three steps before a hand closes on my shoulder. "Young lady!" Then, worse, "Sasha Harless!"

Panic bangs into my chest. I twist free of the officer's grip. I keep pushing on Mikey. "Go! I'll catch up!"

Mikey turns to look at me. His eyes are wide and almost all pupil. I think for a second it's fear, but then he grins—this quick, wild grin that I've never seen on him before—and starts to run again. Now that he's running on his own, I'm having trouble keeping up. Mikey is tiny and built out of muscle, and he's quick as a hummingbird.

I grasp a handful of my cousin's filthy T-shirt, uncertainty wedging itself into my heart. He's going too fast, getting too far ahead of me. I want him to escape, but not alone. I think of Shirley, weeks ago, asking if I could handle him, and I struggle to hold on, but I can't get a good grip. I feel the warmth of his skin through the thin cloth, the sharp jut of his shoulder blade, before my fingertips lose contact.

Mikey does not turn around as he disappears into the woods. One minute, he's in sight, and the next, he isn't anymore. Like everyone else I've ever loved.

21

I've never been in a police station before. I expected ringing phones and jangling jail keys and officers coming in with criminals. Instead it's just me and the officer who caught me. We're sitting on opposite ends of a bench. He has a black eye and a sprained pinkie. He has scratches the shape of my fingernails up and down his arms. He looks heavenward, and then at the clock, and then at me.

"Young lady," he says, then seems to remember that he knows my name. "Miss Harless."

"Where's my cousin?" I ask.

"Well now, Sasha, you're the one that told him to run. So you know as much as I do about where he's gone."

I feel sick. I may have done the wrong thing.

"I didn't *want* him to be by himself, but . . ."

He picks his teeth. "Well, Sasha, nobody wants anything but the best for William." He says *best* slower than the rest of the sentence. He pinches the bridge of his nose, winces. He forgot his black eye. I forget, too, but I know I must have done it. "William's a young boy. He has problems. We all understand that. We just want to find him so we can take care of him."

"His name's Mikey, and he doesn't have any *problems*. He didn't mean anything bad. Running away was my idea," I say.

Officer Cruise shifts his weight and the bench creaks. His brass nametag catches the light. "Sasha," he says. "How 'bout you help us find the boy."

I shift lower in my seat. The wooden bench is warm. I wonder if it is certified Alley Rush hardwood like they were selling at the festival. "I don't know how to find Mikey. He's all alone. He's not very good at running away. I don't know where he is." The truth of it sinks into my stomach. "I don't know where he is."

Grace comes, and looks me up and down to make certain I'm in one piece.

"You do know how to give a body a heart attack," she says. Then she turns to Officer Cruise, and they talk to each other like I'm not here. Once in a while, one of them says something to me in the sort of voice you'd use to get close to a stray cat. I don't hear their words.

I ask for the bathroom. But there aren't any windows. I'm stuck. I sit in the corner of the bathroom. I rock. I worry about Mikey. I think I might be crying.

• • •

I ask about Phyllis. Grace says no. She says someone else has agreed to take me.

"Your cousin's on the way," she says.

"Mikey?"

"Not that cousin." Her voice is kind, but I tune her out. I stand and pace.

"Sasha?"

In the doorway is Hubert Harless. I think for a minute I'm seeing a ghost. But Hubert is wearing his blue flannel shirt and threadbare jeans. If he had died in the mines, his ghost would be stuck forever in his mining uniform. I figure that means he's alive, which is so earthshaking that I need to sit down, except Hubert has crossed the room to me in two steps and put his arms around me. I don't know if he's touching me in anger or relief until he kisses the top of my head.

"Sasha," he says. "God Almighty."

"You're—" I can't say *alive*. I'm afraid he might contradict me.

"You scared me, little lady," he says. I can't bear the kindness in his voice. He has to know.

"I lost Mikey," I rush to confess.

He shushes me. He smells like coal. His hands are so gentle for a man his size.

"Hubert, I lost Mikey."

"We both did, honey," he says.

22

Night comes. Not the good kind. The kind that might not ever get light again. My gaze flies back and forth. First, I look at Hubert, alive. Stuck underground till late in the evening the day of the accident, but alive. Not even hurt. And then I turn my gaze to the window, in case Mikey is out there. Hubert drives past the festival sign. The vendors have stopped selling. Nobody is dancing in the street. Outside of town, along the edges of the woods, you can see the people searching. You can see the deputy badges and the bobbing flashlights. It looks like a miniature hardwood festival, there among the trees.

Hubert says he's taking me home. I throw open the truck door. The ground slices past.

Hubert swerves onto the shoulder of the road. He swears at me. He leans across me to slam the truck door. He says these damn kids will be the death of him yet.

"You're worried about Mikey," I say.

His voice is still shaking. "You're damn right I am."

"It's my fault he's lost." I feel the truth of this to my bones.

"Jesus H. Christ, Sasha, that's no reason to jump out of the doggone truck."

"I'm not leaving Alley Rush until I find him." Till I make up for this stupid thing I've done, dragging Mikey away from Caboose before we knew Hubert was all right.

Hubert swears and swears. When he stops talking, he keeps breathing hard. He hunches over the wheel. This is the closest to crying I've ever seen a coal miner. I tilt my head and study him, but he never looks back at me.

We sit by the road for a full five minutes. Then Hubert turns the truck around.

We watch motel cable. First is a lawyer show and then a teacher show and then a game show. Then Mikey is on a few channels.

Hubert presses "mute" and dials the phone. He swears, clangs the receiver back onto the base. Picks up the phone again and remembers to dial 9 first. He waits a minute. Then he hands the phone to me.

"Hello?" comes a familiar voice. Emotion clogs my throat. There are so many things I have to tell her: I've lost Mikey and I don't get to come home to her and I spent her guitar money. I swallow a couple of times before I speak.

"Oh. Hey, Phyllis, it's me." My words come out normal, but her response isn't.

"Good Lord above," she says, and starts crying.

I wait till she gets a little quieter, and I tell her, "I lost Mikey." I think I ought to still be crying, too, but I've gone dry.

"That little boy's going to turn up," she says. "I promise you, Sasha." Phyllis doesn't seem the type to promise lightly, so this makes me feel a little better.

I have more bad news, though. I tell her, "They won't let you have me again. They found out I have a cousin."

She laughs. "Honey, that's a good thing. Hubert's your family, and I've never seen that man so scared as when you and Mikey turned up missing."

"But I never bought you a GUI-tar, and now they won't let you have me again."

One breath in and another out. Not so steady now.

"I was going to buy you a GUI-tar. I was." In case she doesn't believe me. "I was saving in my suitcase. I picked out the GUI-tar at the pawnshop. It was the pretty one. Three down on the left." In case she wants to buy it herself, except I know Mr. Cardman doesn't pay her that much.

"The suitcase," she says. Her voice sounds damp. "Oh, Sasha. I thought you were saving to make your escape."

I don't know what to say to that, because I *did* make my escape with the money. I don't say anything at all. I feel like I did something wrong by letting her think that. I want to apologize, but I don't know how. And then I feel like I did something wrong by saving up for something other than escape. Like if Michael were here, he would disapprove of my priorities. I've got so many different kinds of guilt in my heart tonight. I fold up on the motel bed, sitting on my knees with my forehead pressed into the pillows.

Phyllis keeps talking to me, managing to sound almost normal. She tells me everything is going to be all right. She tells me over and over. I can't find my voice again, so I cling to hers. My breathing starts to hitch. When we are one *all right* short of me bursting into tears, I get up and hand the phone to Hubert. I lie down on the bed.

"It's me," Hubert says into the phone. "Yeah. Yeah, I think she's okay."

I roll onto my side. I close my eyes. Hubert talks to Phyllis until after I'm asleep.

I'm quick to wake, but it takes a long time to remember where I am. And then, all at once, that I don't know where Mikey might be. He's only nine. He won't admit he's still afraid of the dark.

The motel room smells like old cigarette smoke and something clean that I can't quite name. It's empty except for me. I find Hubert smoking and pacing on the balcony. The morning is already warm and humid. There are no cars coming or going. I see us reflected at odd angles in the windows that stretch away down the row. Hubert's reflection is broad and solid. I steal a glance at him and find he doesn't look as broad or as solid when you can see his face. His curly beard and mustache hide most of his expression, but the worry lines around his brown eyes are tough to hide.

The motel curtains are closed. I think of the empty beds behind them. I think of sleeping in grass, in a field, in the rain. I think of Mikey sleeping somewhere, somewhere.

"Morning," Hubert says.

He stops pacing and leans on his elbows on the balcony railing. I lean on my elbows on the balcony railing, too. We look out at the quiet parking lot. We shake our heads. We exhale slowly.

We look for Mikey high and low. We look for him in the woods. We look for him in the city. The police are looking. The people of Alley Rush are looking. But I know that if anyone finds him, it will be us.

I wish I had Michael's worry stone with me. I pick up a piece of gravel and roll it between my fingers as we search. I wish I had given Mikey the suitcase. I would feel better if he had some money. Some crackers. The last of the peanut butter. I wish I had a poem for this.

I try:

> *Mikey went away.*
> *Me and Hubert waited, but—*

I stop. I try:

Mikey.
Small, sweet.
sad beyond sad,
lost in the coalfields.

I stop. The last time I did poetry, I convinced Mikey that running away was a good idea. Now he's missing. There is no form for this. There are no words for this.

The pictures in my head are these:
Mikey asleep in a field in the rain.
Mikey asleep in the woods under a tree.
Mikey dead.
Mikey crying because he's hungry.
Mikey crying because he's scared.
Mikey dead.
Mikey how he looks back home. Moping on his porch. Running from the shed.
Mikey how he looks back home. Stirring up muffins. Greasing the tin. Tilting his head like he'll never understand me.
Hubert talks while he drives. I listen to his voice, and my breath, and rain on the roof of the truck. I can hear the truck seat creaking while I rock.
We drive from one end of Alley Rush to the other. We

take note of roads that look inviting. We drive up one road and down the next. We forget to eat. We study the roadside. We check under bridges, in culverts, in old, leaning red school bus houses. We sneak into yards and check under front porches. We see a lot of empty things.

"You done this before?" I ask Hubert. It doesn't really come out sounding like a question.

"Mikey's momma could have done better than me," Hubert says by way of answer. His fingers wrap and unwrap on the steering wheel for a minute. "I was already pushing thirty when we got married. She was younger. Nineteen. Pretty as a picture."

"What if the picture's ugly?"

"Huh?"

"That saying. I don't get it. Can't somebody be pretty as an ugly picture?"

Hubert snorts, shakes his head. "Nah. Aster was pretty as a very pretty picture. I still don't know why she married me, unless it was the job. She had a thing for coal miners."

"Why?"

He snorts again. "You got something against coal miners?"

I charge ahead before I can hurt his feelings. "I just mean 'cause you're gone all day and you come home really tired. Wouldn't she rather have a thing for, I don't know, news anchors? They get to dress nice, and they don't usually die at their jobs."

Hubert steers past a downed tree limb. "Coal miners don't usually die at their jobs," he says.

"Sometimes they do."

"Sometimes people die no matter what they do for a living." He glances at me. "Honey, I know you lost people. Hell, we all lost people. But folks still got to turn the lights on and that means we need coal and that means we need miners. And folks still need to put out fires, and that means we got to have guys like your brother. Ain't anything in this world that's totally safe. A person might as well do the thing he loves."

"Do you love what you do?"

He pumps the brake, steers across the yellow line to avoid the crumbling edges of the highway. Slows to avoid oncoming cars. "I do," he says. Then, quieter, "Or what passes for love in a guy like me."

It seems an odd thing to say, especially for a man with three children and at least two wives that I know of. "But you loved Aster, right?"

"Yes, ma'am. I did love Aster." There is sadness but no doubt in his voice.

"And you love Mikey. You love Sara and Marla."

"Of course I do."

"And you love Shirley."

"Sure. I love Shirley." His foot finds the gas, and the truck speeds up a little. We drive awhile in silence before I hear Hubert repeat, in a low voice, like it's meant for only himself to hear, "Or what passes for love in a guy like me."

The closer day gets to night, the more scared I feel. I know Mikey can get through one night by himself; one night by himself might be all right. But this will be two nights by himself. This will be two cold, long, dark nights with Mikey alone in the woods trying to figure out what to do next. I know he doesn't know. I know he is worse than I am, even, at surviving in the wild.

Night falls like glass. The storm breaks. Lightning and thunder. Downpour like a faucet turned on.

We're in the motel parking lot, but I won't get out of the truck. I'll stay right here, where I can look for Mikey.

Hubert pushes out a frustrated breath. He sits beside me for a while. Then he gets out of the truck. A rush of cooler air sweeps in. I smell damp pavement. I grip the seam of the upholstery. I curl my toes onto the seat.

Hubert brings a motel blanket to the truck. He tucks me in. He sits beside my head where it rests on the seat. He turns the key in the ignition so we can have radio. There are country songs, weather, reports about the search for a missing boy. Hubert turns the key the other way. The windows won't roll up all the way, and rain drips in through the cracks. I curl my feet up tighter to keep them dry. Hubert leans his head against the window.

"You asked if I done this before," Hubert says after a while. His voice is soft against the rain. "You know about Mikey's mama, right?"

I think of the papers we found. "She got sick," I say. I don't like to say the words that were on the paper, words like *toxicology screen* and *treatment for addiction*.

"She got real sick," Hubert confirms. "And she ran off with Mikey."

I sit up and twist around to look at him. "She took Mikey with her?"

Hubert doesn't look at me. His gaze is fixed on something past the windshield, something far away, out in the night. "Three days," he said. "I knew she was struggling, but . . . it's your wife, you know? You want to think she's okay. Then she took off with my boy. He was only five. Three days they was missing." He shakes his head slowly, closing his eyes. I study his weathered, wrinkled skin and his heavy mustache and beard. I wonder if he keeps all that facial hair to hide behind at times like this. But I can see behind it anyway, all the lines that must have got there in those three days, and all the lines that are deepening tonight.

"Where'd they go?" I ask when he gets quiet too long. I wish Mikey'd felt like he could tell me some of this.

He shakes his head. "Mikey never would say. I got him back when she checked herself into the hospital."

Now I twist to look at him again. "She checked herself in?"

"She was real sick, Sasha. I think she knew . . . well, I think she wanted to get clean. For Mikey."

"Well, how come Mikey didn't know, then? I mean . . . I mean, he got really upset when we found the hospital papers."

Hubert shakes his head. "He was a little thing, Sasha. He knew he went on an adventure with his mother. He always just thought I went and got him back. He didn't understand what was happening. He didn't know how sick she was."

"It was . . . it was drugs, right?"

"Yes, it was."

"I don't understand why people do that."

Hubert runs a hand down his face. "Because they got to do something. Life just piles up and piles up until they can't hack it. They got to make it stop somehow." His words make me think of Chris McKenzie, whose death sent me running out to the Dumpster that day at school. I think of sparks floating up above the parking lot at the Save-Great, of the way he played with fire so he didn't have to stop and deal with things. I didn't know Chris. Can't remember his face very well. In my head, he looks a little like Michael. I might have been the last person to see him alive, lighting things on fire because he had to do *something*.

"What could pile up so bad that Aster would leave you like that?"

Hubert lets out this awful noise, halfway between a sigh and a sob, before he answers. "There was a lot of hurt in Aster's life," he says. "And she didn't have . . ." He draws this funny little picture in the air with his hands, like he just can't find the right words to explain. "She didn't have the right kind of mind to deal with all that hurt. So she had to find a way to make it stop hurting, and the way she found was drugs."

I look from Hubert's face to the ceiling of the truck, headliner sagging and stuck up with thumbtacks. I think about what Hubert's telling me, and this feeling swims up in me, this horrifying feeling that I shouldn't be having, this feeling that might be envy.

"Why'd she take him?"

"Well, she loved him, Sasha."

"Why'd she take him and Judy didn't take me?" Hubert twists in his seat to look at me.

"Judy left when I was five. And she wasn't sick. She felt like a caged bird who wanted to get free. Why didn't she take me?" I think of what my life would be like if my mother had taken me with her all those years ago. I wouldn't have had to wait for news of Ben's death. I wouldn't have had to watch Michael be lowered into the ground. I think of all the places my big brother wanted me to see, how much work he put into making sure I would see them. I think how maybe our mother has seen them all already. She could have saved Michael so much worry and trouble, and she could have saved me from all these sad things.

"Do you wish she had taken you?" Hubert asks. "What about your dad and your brother? What would they have done without you?"

I think of Frisbee in the graveyard with Michael. I think of rowdy housecleaning days set to loud music. There would have been no arm wrestling and hugs from Ben, no kisses hello and good-bye when he came home and left again for the mines. There would have been no poetry club. No finger-bone muffins with Mikey and no four a.m. egg salad with Phyllis.

But I would never have met Mikey. I latch onto that thought.

"She should have taken me with her," I say, "so I wouldn't have had the chance to lose Mikey." I've never felt as terrible about anything as I do right now about this.

Hubert sighs and lets his arm drape across me. "Try to get some sleep, little lady," he says in a low, rough voice. I close my eyes.

In the morning, I help Hubert gather up the blanket to drag it into the motel. "Paid for a whole room and used one blanket," Hubert mutters. "Danged expensive blanket if you ask me."

In the bathroom, I look at the mirror. The glass is smooth. I don't look past it at the girl in the reflection.

We climb into the truck. But it takes a long time for Hubert to turn the key. It takes a long time for Hubert to put the truck into drive. It takes a long time for Hubert to press the gas and aim us toward the road.

When we search in the direction of Caboose, my heart beats faster. My breath gets louder. I'm most calm when we search the other direction, toward Beckley and the rest of the world.

We see a lot of the area today. We see more yellow ribbons tied on more power poles. We see more signs, in store windows and out front of churches: OUR PRAYERS ARE WITH THE DOGWOOD FAMILY and PRAY FOR OUR COAL MINERS and WE LOVE OUR MINORS, which is spelled wrong, which makes it fit both my situations but still makes me want to cry.

"What happened the other day?" I ask.

Hubert's scanning the tree line. "Which day?" he asks. "You're going to have to be a little more specific."

"At work." He's told me the basics—that he was stuck a few hours and he never got hurt—but the ribbons and the signs in Alley Rush let me know there's more to the story.

"Oh," he says.

"There's all these ribbons."

"Yeah." His voice is sad. "Freak accident. Couldn't have been avoided."

"Did people die?"

He swallows, hard. "Two, probably. They ain't found them yet. Two more got hurt."

"Why do you go back?"

"It's my job."

"Hubert, I don't get it. That makes five people killed this year."

"It ain't usually like that, Sasha."

"So just every *few* years, a bunch of people die?"

"If you don't get it, then you just don't." Hubert sounds exasperated. He tugs at his mustache and his voice softens. "I don't mean you, Sash. I mean everybody. People think it's crazy, that we're hillbillies back in the mountains digging coal because we don't know no better. They wouldn't last a day. You got to be smart and know your sh—stuff. The equipment, the training—it's not some dumb hillbilly job. My dad worked the strip job. He was the explosives guy. You know how precise you got to be to handle explosives?" He glances sideways, seems to realize who he's talking to. "I mean, no, I don't reckon you do. Least you better not." Half a smile. "I've worked the strip job and I've been underground, and the only thing I can tell you is, I love my job. Every time I flip on the damn light, I think, *I did that*. What would this place be without the guy in my job?"

"But if something bad happens to the guy in your job, where would his family be?" I sneak a hand across the truck seat until my pinkie and Hubert's pinkie are close enough to touch.

He looks at me again, quick and startled, and then at the road, and then back at me.

"Well, shoot, Sasha," he says. "I ain't got an easy answer for you on that one."

We see houses in town that lean toward each other like they're cheating on a test. Kids' bicycles and plastic turtle-shaped sandboxes and electric scooters litter yards while their eight-year-old owners sit on the steps, playing with handheld video games. Teenage girls walk together in groups of three or four, passing cigarettes back and forth. Boys shove each other and gas up their four-wheelers. Women wrestle babies into loud trucks with big tires and cutout silhouettes of coal miners taking up the rear windows, stickers that read COAL MINER'S WIFE or COAL MINER'S DAUGHTER.

We leave town. Outside it, there is space between the houses. Trailers climb hills like mountain goats. Pit bulls and German shepherds pace grooves around the trees they're chained to. There are still kids' bicycles and plastic turtle-shaped sandboxes.

Farther out, there are cows, and tired horses with sharp backbones. There's a rooster standing on a barn roof. There's a shiny green tractor stuck in the mud. There are half a dozen leaning grain silos, ribs showing, siding worn through. There's an eerie blank spot against the sky, an abandoned screen from a drive-in theater that closed more than a decade ago, back when this used to be a town. Every few miles, a low-slung building covered in dead vines of ivy claims a wide spot next to the road, windows boarded up and peppered with buckshot from somebody's target practice. Nothing has been open for miles, not even the front doors of houses.

We keep driving until there's nothing but road, with a steep climb on one side and a drop-off on the other. Trees reach across the road to touch branches over top. With all the leaves leaning low, the sky never seems to get all the way light, even when there is sun.

We stop searching long enough to head back to the motel for lunch. Hubert insists. He says Grace will take me away if I'm not fed. He says he's supposed to be my temporary guardian and a temporary guardian at the very least makes sure the temporarily guarded is fed.

We're almost to town when Hubert slams on the brakes. He curses and punches the wheel. There is a truck jackknifed in the road up ahead. The traffic snakes away in front of us, a sea of brake lights. Nobody is moving. Fear comes up in me so quick I can't contain it. *We are all stuck. We are all stuck. We are all stuck.*

I panic. I aim to move the glass.

In case I get upset again, Hubert requires me to wait at the motel. This is not an ideal situation, he says. Who knows what trouble I might get into at the motel? But I have to wait somewhere, and he has to look for Mikey. We're three days out, and every day he's missing, he gets that much harder to find. Hubert says a few other choice words, too, mostly to himself and mostly words I'm not supposed to say. I can't tell exactly whether he's angry or whether he's just upset and overwhelmed like I was in the car when I started trying to fight my way out. I didn't make a dent in the windshield, of course, but I reopened the cut on my hand. Hubert wraps it up clumsily for me before he starts to leave.

He's halfway out the door when I start crying, snot-nosed, hiccupping, out-loud bawling. I don't see it coming and am caught midstep between the TV and the bed. I think I was reaching for the remote.

We wait until Phyllis arrives in her little car. It rises when she climbs out of it. She hugs Hubert in the parking lot. She talks quietly to him. She climbs the steps. I stare at my reflection in the window. Tangled hair. Tangled brow.

Phyllis comes in softly and hugs me. I'm all right until I see that she has brought egg salad. Egg salad is for front porches and four a.m. It's for mornings when Mikey will be out in an hour. I shove the egg salad into the trash can. I fall onto her shoulder and grip a handful of her shirt. She smooths my back over and over and whispers, "Sweet Sasha."

Phyllis orders us a pizza without mentioning the cost or the wasted sandwiches. While we wait, she washes my face. She lays the washcloth against my neck. She digs a brush from her purse and works on my hair. She runs down to her car and brings back some of my clothes, old and worn and clean.

"Take a shower, love," she says. "Get into something fresh."

I sit. I think of Mikey's torn jeans. I think of Mikey filthy. I think, *My fault my fault my fault*. I think I don't deserve to be clean.

"You'll feel better," Phyllis coaxes. She goes into the bathroom. I can see her in the mirror, turning on the shower, testing the temperature. She fluffs a towel twice, three times, with shaky hands. She looks like she'll feel better if I take the shower, so I do. I have a hard time breaking the seal on the tiny shampoo bottles with the motel logo on them. My hands have no strength behind them. I think of Phyllis, the first time I saw her hands after her GUI-tar was broken. I think of holding Mikey's hand, pulling him along. I think of tossing the Frisbee with Michael, wrestling the remote from him. I think of my hands thumb-wrestling with Ben, holding his hand when I was little. I flex my fingers. Hands can be tired from not doing the things they want to do.

I stand in the shower. I count the seconds. Each slow second, each stubborn second, I will myself to be in some other place, some other time, but nothing happens except my fingers get pruny. So many seconds go by, I forget how to stop. I lose myself in the counting. I don't know what comes next. I don't know what comes next. I don't know what comes next.

23

In the middle of the night, without opening my eyes, I ask, "What if we don't find him?"

Hubert sighs, and I hear the bedsprings and his knees creak as he sinks onto the other bed.

"It's two in the morning, little lady."

"He's not with his mom. She's not there to bring him back. What if he never comes back, Hubert? What if I lost him for real?" Now I crack an eye open to look at him. In the light of the TV he's left on for distraction, he looks old and gray.

"That boy was lost long before you came along," Hubert says. "I think you found a little piece of him I never could."

"What do you mean? What piece?"

"The piece that smiles." I see Hubert's mustache twitch. I remember Mikey saying he laughed a lot in Caboose, but

I know it isn't true. At least, not *real* laughs, at something more than a gross scene in a movie or a joke you've played on someone.

"Did he smile a lot?" I ask. "You know—before his mom?"

"He was a silly kid. Always laughing and running off to get into things. Probably part of why Aster couldn't stay away with him more than a couple of days. She was having trouble keeping him up. Keeping him, you know, safe and all." He tugs his mustache, hard. Works his jaw. "She could see herself sometimes. Just every once in a while. She could see . . . well, it was like the mirror always had the sun caught in it and all she could see was its reflection, blinding. Then, every once in a while, there'd come a cloud over top, and she'd see herself the way she really was. Skinny and sick . . ." He rolls away from me.

I think of how Ben missed Judy for years, even though she left. I take a chance on a question that's none of my business. "How can you love Aster and Shirley both?"

He's quiet so long, I think he's gone to sleep. But then he says, "I love 'em different, Sasha."

"Different how?"

"It's two in the morning," he repeats. "Go to sleep, little lady."

I think of Shirley and her apple kitchen, her dishpan hands, her two little girls born barely a year apart.

"Does Shirley know you love 'em different?"

"God." The word is more breath than voice. "You sure have some questions, you know that?"

"I just don't get it."

"Lord, Sasha, nobody gets it. It's just—it's how it works, you know? Everybody you love, you're gonna love different. Only I didn't know . . . I didn't know *how* different before I married Shirley." He coughs his smoker's cough a couple of times. "She's a good woman, Sasha. I know she's got her faults. We all got our faults. But she's a good woman. She deserves better than . . ." He clears his throat. "It's two in the damn morning, Sasha. Get some sleep."

But I don't. I slip out of bed and cross the room to Hubert; give him the quickest of pecks on the cheek.

"Night," I say before retreating to my own bed.

Startled, he looks after me with grim eyes and a kind smile. "Night, Sash."

24

They call off the search at the start of June, a week after Mikey disappeared into the woods. They say, *We're still looking for your son.* They say, *This doesn't mean you should give up hope.* And while they talk, they call the teams in out of the forest. Weary Alley Rush folks dust themselves off and head into their houses, chins low, shoulders stooped. They say, *We wanted this to have a happy ending.* They say, *Everybody wanted this to have a happy ending.*

They can't stay in the woods forever. I understand that. But I think they could have stayed in the woods another five minutes, and then another five minutes, and then another five minutes. How do they know they aren't that close to finding Mikey? They could be giving up fifteen minutes short of bringing my cousin home safe.

He might not be in the Alley Rush area anymore, the police tell Hubert. *He might have made it to the next town. Or maybe somebody picked him up.* Hubert winces. *We've got a missing child alert out nationwide. We've got his face all over. We can't keep these men in the woods; their families need them.*

This is the first time that I can tell, truly and without a doubt, that Hubert is my cousin. We don't talk. He doesn't talk and I don't talk. We stare at the police officer's pale green eyes until he closes them, looks away, studies his knuckles. We don't have to talk; I know he hears us. We have family that needs us, too.

It is true, though, that every square inch of the woods around Alley Rush has been searched. Mikey isn't there. He isn't anywhere.

Shirley says Hubert has to go back to work, and Grace says I have to go back to school. There are only a handful of days left, and I need to take my tests. We don't care about work and school, but Shirley and Grace have ways of making us do things we don't want to do.

We drive down and down. I watch the sky get grayer, the trees get grittier, the night get darker. Lighted windows up toward Alley Rush look bright and warm, but the closer we get to Caboose, the dimmer the lighted windows look. Some of the windows still have their heavy plastic up from winter, and the lights behind them are blurry. I watch clean cars give way to filthy trucks. I watch sidewalks give way to train tracks.

We crunch onto the shoulder at the end of the lawn, and Hubert shuts off the engine. I hear forest sounds, thick and heavy, birds and crickets. After a week at the motel in Alley Rush, it's odd to hear forest sounds in the middle of town. I look at the trees all around us. I think if we had carved them up like the people of Alley Rush, we wouldn't be able to hear woods sounds now. I feel like a stranger, like a traveler. I feel an odd relief to be home.

I won't get out of the truck. I won't go inside the house, go to sleep in a bed, eat food. I won't allow life to continue without Mikey. I won't get out of the truck. I won't.

Except Marla and Sara are on the porch. Sara looks older, just in the week we've spent away. She's growing to look more like her mother all the time. Marla takes after Hubert with her round face that is almost always a breath away from smiling.

I itch to hold the babies, to tickle under their arms until they squeal, to hold them tight while they fall asleep on my shoulder. I get out of the truck.

I try to will Mikey to be waiting on the porch. I will him to find his way home. But I don't think Mikey could find home if he wanted. He followed me through the woods on our way out. He followed *me*, not the creek, not the highway. It won't occur to him to turn around, to retrace the highway to the creek, to retrace the creek to our front porches. Even if it did occur to him, I made my case. I talked him out of ever coming home just a few hours before he vanished. If he's looking for me, this is the last place he'd expect to find me.

Hubert asks me where I want my things. Am I okay sharing a room with the babies? Sleeping in Mikey's bed? Or would I rather sleep on the couch? Would I rather be in a space by myself even if it's the couch? I forgot I don't live with Phyllis anymore. Phyllis is the neighbor. She's not my foster parent anymore. Upstairs in her house is an empty bedroom and, if I know her, a perfectly made bed with an old quilt smoothed on top. She's waiting for another borrowed kid, waiting for a new, maybe not so drastic set of problems. She is waiting to teach somebody else how to cook.

I hurt for Michael. The county watched us, but there was no worry about them taking me away and giving Michael some other kid. Michael and I were bound by blood and everything we'd lost. We watched our mother walk away. We waited for our dad to come back. We were connected in ways I will never be connected to anybody else.

And now there is no Michael.

And there is no Mikey.

I am connected to no one.

I am still staring at Hubert, and he is waiting for my answer. I can't begin to imagine taking Mikey's bed.

"The couch," I say.

Shirley takes Marla from me when we walk into the house. She has lines around her mouth.

I see Sara mimic her frown. I kiss the top of Sara's head.

Shirley changes Marla while I follow Sara, picking up the things she's dropped on the floor—her shoes, her pants, the hair bow Shirley insists on. There's a trail of freedom behind Sara. She doesn't like to be stuck, even in clothes. I gather up her stuff and make a pile on the nightstand. Immediately, Marla appears to scavenge.

"Sossa," she says. It's as close as she can get to my name. I think it sounds like *salsa*, and it makes me smile. She's talking more than she was even a week ago. She tugs her loose diaper up with her free hand and stands on her tippy-toes. I lean over so she can kiss my cheek, a sloppy, wet little smack.

"Ew, you're yucky," I tease.

"Gucky." She beams and sticks a finger in her nose. I guess somebody's told her one too many times that nose-picking is yucky, and now she thinks that's what *yucky* means.

"Yeah, that's gucky, too. Quit that." I tug her hand away

from her nose and tickle her under the armpit. She folds sideways with a shriek.

"Don't get them girls rowdied up before bedtime," Shirley says from the door.

I rush to stand. "Sorry." I don't know how to act in Shirley's house. It's so strange to be here at night and without Mikey.

"Sleep tight," Shirley says when she hands me blankets for the couch. "Hubert, you gonna read to them girls?"

I don't recognize the book, but it sounds sweet and far away. I lie in the next room and stare at the ceiling with its long cracks from the cold and its low-hanging bulb with no cover. The blanket scratching my skin smells like cigarette smoke. The couch is lumpy in a specific pattern. My feet are in a groove where Shirley must sit. My hips are down even lower in Hubert's spot. The rest of me is on firm cushion where the girls don't make a dent. And there's a rip above my head. Mikey's place.

After the story stops, and I hear Hubert clumping away into his room, Shirley's voice rattles out, hopping mad about something. I hear my name. I hear the back-and-forth of their voices without hearing any words. There is never a point where I hear the voices stop, but eventually I realize they have.

I roll over. The apple-shaped night-light from the kitchen sketches shadows on the floor. The carpet is flat and dull from years of feet. It's the same brown as river mud. I can see the nail holes in the wood underneath where the carpet is torn away in one corner.

I roll the other way. The house settles. The wind rattles the sheets of plastic Hubert still hasn't taken off the windows from when the house got too cold in winter. Shirley's computer stops whirring and goes into sleep mode.

I was waiting for everything to be silent, but old houses never are. So I wait, at least, for all the people to fall silent.

I get up and walk out into the backyard. I stand outside Mikey's window. I stare in at the little girls, lumps of sleepy blanket in their beds. Their night-light is shaped like a butterfly. I miss Mikey on the other side of the glass. I miss the last time I saw him, filthy, running, hungry. I miss the first time I saw him, scared, silent.

I stand at the window and wait.

Phyllis comes out at four a.m. It ought to surprise me that she knows where to find me, but it doesn't. I guess she already knew about me and Mikey staring at each other in the dark. She leads me to her porch, where the sandwiches are.

"I'm up," she says. "I'll help you get ready for school. Hubert's a dear, God love him, but he don't know how to get a teenage girl ready for school."

I let Stella climb onto my lap and share my sandwich.

I let Phyllis unbraid my hair. I trust her to braid it back again. She does, after a long, slow brushing. She braids it tight, ties new ribbon over the rubber bands. She hands me new clothes. Black jeans without any holes and a girlie-cut, V-neck pink T-shirt. They are clean and smell like someone else's home.

"Grace sent some things," she says. "They showed up . . . well . . . you wasn't here when they showed up."

I go into her house, which is so familiar it hurts me to walk through it. In the dark, it's silent, breathless, empty. It's changed so much in the week since I was last here. I hear the quiet where I guess there used to be noise pouring down from upstairs, all the sounds of me. I think about how much more peaceful the house must be without me in it.

I hurry up the stairs, shower quick because it's too cold in the house. It might be the beginning of June, but down here between the mountains, it's still spring. When I'm dressed, I peek into my old bedroom. I'm surprised to find my bed unmade. I want so badly to crawl inside it, but instead I stand and look at it. I don't fit there anymore.

"Hubert said to tell you good-bye," Phyllis says from the door. "He left for work."

She comes into the room, holds me at arm's length so she can look me up and down. "You look real pretty in that outfit," she says.

"Do you think Mikey's dead?" The words taste so awful that I wish I hadn't said them, but now they're hanging out in the open, waiting to be dealt with.

Phyllis presses me close to her for a long moment. "No," she says. "I do not."

I don't speak to Jaina on the bus. She talks for a while, and then she stops. She crisscrosses her boots at the ankle.

"Are you mad at me?" she asks.

I feel exhausted. I wish she knew it's not her I'm mad at; it's me. But I don't have the energy to explain. I am silent, like I used to be before poetry club. I wait and I wait for this day to be done.

After English class, Miss Jacks stops me at her desk and speaks quietly. Her voice is like a poem without an ending. She wavers into silence, waiting for a rhythm that doesn't come. She is a haiku without the last five syllables, a cinquain without the final synonym. She does not get anything from me.

Anthony stops me outside of class. He puts a warm hand on my cold arm. He doesn't seem to notice his uncomfortable-looking friends nearby, all of them dressed like he is, in saggy pants and slouchy shirts, with their hair growing long. He ducks to look at my eyes. His own are large and darker blue than usual. He asks, "Any word on your cousin?"

There are several words on my cousin. *Lost. Scared. Hurt. Troubled.* I don't want to say any of them out loud. I stare at Anthony's face until the lines blur, until I can't see his concern, until I can't feel his concern. His hand loses its grip, slides up my arm and then off my shoulder as I pass him, like I did at the Dumpsters last year, willing him not to see me.

In a town like ours, there are bad things, and there are shared bad things.

Shared bad things are big, like a bad storm or a flood. Sometimes a car accident with a lot of cars involved. Or, once every few years, bad news from the mine. From the first flashing light, the first wailing siren, the people of this town pull together, circle the wagons, protect each other. Everybody speaks in half sentences—*"So young"* or *"God's will"* or *"A real shame"*—because everybody knows the other half of the story.

When bad things happen only to one family, it feels different. Still, everybody knows. Still, everybody has heard about your cousin skipping town and disappearing in the woods. Everybody has heard about you and the boy's father, the two of you clueless, searching and searching. They murmur. They use complete sentences: *"Bless their hearts"* and *"You think he'll turn up?"*

I close myself to the murmurs. I close myself to the

talk. I close myself to the little voices who think they know what I'm going through.

I sit on the bench in Town Center. I look at the yellow ribbons. I wonder where Mikey's flowers are. Before I leave, I thread my fingers through a handful of purple clovers and yellow dandelions. They come up by the root. Tendrils reach down through clumps of dirt like fingers trying to hold on. I knock the mud out of their grip. I spill them across the steps of the caboose, where they will wilt and die by morning.

25

Hubert doesn't look like himself when he hasn't been in the mines. He's too clean and he's not wearing coveralls. Of course, he's still in jeans and flannel, so I can still tell it's him. But he's off somehow. His eyes are different. Squintier. He tugs at his beard all the time.

"He may have"—except he pronounces it like *may of*—"got seen in Beckley," he says. "I'll drive up that way after dinner."

Shirley looks up from her plate of burnt cube steak. It's the first week of summer vacation. We're eating dinner too early, since Hubert has been home today. It's barely five. We usually eat later, seven or eight, sometimes even nine if Hubert is late getting home. "To Beckley? Tonight?"

"I'll go with you," I say.

Hubert nods. I sag with relief. He could easily say no. He could easily say I'm too much trouble.

Shirley goes back to her plate. Her face is gathered like fabric around a pulled thread.

"We don't got a lot of money for gas," she says, but she says it quiet, like she doesn't expect an answer. I glace up at her quickly and then at the girls, but nobody seems to notice me.

Sara is singing a song about the cube steak. She makes it up as she goes along. "This is my dinner, my dinner is *good*! This is my dinner, my dinner is *yummy*! This is my dinner, my dinner is *awesome*!" Her words all blur together like she isn't sure where one ends and the next begins.

"Awesome," Marla repeats, sticking her fingers in Sara's plate. Sara screeches and slaps her sister's fingers. Marla wails, but nobody pays any attention. Hubert is staring past the girls, toward Beckley. Shirley stabs the meat so hard her fork hits the plate with a shriek.

Hubert turns to look at Shirley. "What do you expect me to do?" His voice is just a little louder, just a little faster, than usual. Marla keeps grabbing for things from Sara's plate, but Sara is staring at her father now. Her gaze darts rabbit-quick to me and then back to Hubert.

"I expect you to go get him. Of course I expect you to go get him." And I believe her. Her face is so tired. But something's still wrong.

"I could find him tonight," Hubert says. "I could get him home."

"I know, Hugh. I know. You need to go."

215

"Then what—"

"Nothing." She stands quickly, scraping her chair back, and tips her dinner into the disposal. "I want you to find him. I want him home safe. Marla, no." The baby, dry of tears now, is trying to feed Sara fistfuls of mashed potatoes, and her sister is dodging.

Hubert stands, too, and rescues Sara from her sister, planting her on his hip and kissing the side of her face. He can't seem to get enough of hugging and holding the girls since Mikey's been gone.

"I'm just worried," Shirley says. "We got so many bills and you've missed so many days. I'm just worried if you're not at work tomorrow . . ." But she dusts her hands off over the sink and nods sharply before unbuckling Marla from her high chair. "But we can worry about that later."

The way she says it sounds odd. I know Hubert notices, too, because we look at each other and back at her. But she takes the baby to change, leaving us behind her.

Every time Hubert's truck tops a mountain, I think we're there. But Beckley still slips up on me, a slow thickening of the houses by the road. I've been to Beckley plenty of times, but I was a lot younger. I thought it would be more familiar, but either it or I have changed.

Hubert talks to the police for a minute. There's a lot of nodding and a lot of pointing and a whole big lot of frowning. Afterward, my cousin climbs back in the truck.

He puts it in gear and rolls away from the police, who have already turned to attend to other matters.

"He was saw for sure," Hubert says, and he drives us onto brick streets. "A fellow from Alley Rush picked him up walking and tried to take him to the police. Mikey ducked the guy and ran. Headed this way, s'posedly."

"He was found for a minute?" I think about this. For a whole chunk of time, Mikey wasn't missing anymore. Mikey ducked and ran. Mikey wants to be missing. This is scary, this is upsetting, this is—this is really good news. As of this morning, Mikey was alive and well and ducking Good Samaritans. My heart soars.

I think we're going to head home, but then Hubert pulls us over to the curb. As I follow him out of the truck, I scan the sidewalks. It's nearly nine, but it's so warm and summery out that no one has headed inside yet. People are laughing, talking, bringing their dogs out for a last quick walk. It seems an odd place for a nine-year-old to be lost. Everybody looks happy. They are cleaner here than farther south, and there are fewer people wearing reflective coveralls.

The town is pretty this evening. We have to step out of the road to avoid a fast-moving Hummer. Immediately I trip into a group of college students walking together. This town is faster and busier than I'm used to. I wonder how Mikey feels about it, whether it excites or frightens him.

"Excuse me," Hubert says to the college students, who

walk away after giving me an irritated look. They walk faster when Hubert speaks, like maybe we're going to kidnap them or ask them for loose change.

"There's a missing child," I blurt. "Wait!"

They stop and wait like I've asked, but they don't move any closer. They're carrying backpacks too big for them. They look like they're in a hurry.

"This is him," Hubert says, pulling out a picture of Mikey. It's one of those school pictures nobody likes. It says "Proof Copy" diagonally across the middle.

The students look, shake their heads. "Sorry." They scurry away. "Good luck," one of them adds over her shoulder. Her backpack swings.

We walk the opposite direction so they won't think they're being followed. We show Mikey's picture to everybody we find. The people in town all have sympathy because they've seen him on TV, and ideas about where he might be hiding because they know the area, and stories about how one time a kid was missing and turned up safe a hundred miles away, or walked all the way back home on his own, or never came back and it's a shame. None of the stories help, and they take up precious time, but Hubert never rushes. He nods thoughtfully and lets each person speak.

We wave Mikey's picture until it's too dark to see it and the number of people on the sidewalk dwindles to almost zero. We have covered blocks and blocks of town.

If Mikey were with us, I would have loved to walk around the town like this.

"Did anybody check the hospital?" I ask Hubert as we climb into the truck.

"All the hospitals know to look for him," Hubert says.

"I mean . . . I mean his mom's hospital," I say, remembering the papers we found in the box in the shed, the ones from when his mom went into treatment.

"They been on lookout," he says. "But it don't matter."

"Why not?"

"Aster ain't there anymore. Hasn't been for some time. She ran off again a long time ago." He curses, and lights up a cigarette. "He's his mother's son, that's for sure."

We look for Mikey in Beckley the next three days. And we pester his mother's hospital for news of a possible sighting. Now that we know Mikey was headed in this direction, it seems to make sense that maybe he's trying to find his mother. He knows where the hospital is from the papers we found from her treatment. And he's my cousin. He's a lot like me. He would want to find family if he could.

Thursday night is when I give up. This is the night we stay in Beckley till after ten, taping Mikey's serious little face to all the telephone poles. I watch people walk past the poles without looking. I realize we won't find him this way. Later, I lie perfectly still on the lumpy couch. I lie on top of the blanket Shirley gave me. I put my fingers in my ears until everyone is quiet. I lie awake.

Maybe he got to his mother's hospital by now, without being seen somehow. Maybe he found out about his mother, how she ran away. How she disappeared in the night like mothers do. I'm relieved that he's alive. But I can't help thinking, if he does know about his mom, then this is a night when he needs somebody. A dad or a cousin. Somebody. By now he might know that his mother is gone. That she's slipped through his fingers and he will probably never see her again.

He will *never* see her again.

I know I'm being stupid. I know that if Mikey reached the hospital, somebody would have called us. Somebody would have caught him.

At midnight, I slip off the couch. I ease myself through the quiet house one footstep at a time. I open the front door slow enough it doesn't creak. I slip out into the darkness.

I walk until the moon has crossed my narrow wedge of sky and dropped out of sight past the trees. As the sky darkens, I stop outside a closed, narrow storefront with its windows and doors boarded up. The smell of wet, burnt wood is faint but still present.

Something rustles in the shadows. I stop walking toward the ruins and wait for it to be something scary. Instead it's a cat, a lanky tabby with glowing eyes. It meows a warning and then slinks away.

I slink away, too. My feet take me down familiar roads. I climb the stairs from the Dumpster again, let myself into the empty apartment I used to share with Michael. I'm not scared of the dark apartment this time. I can make it past the kitchen, into the pitch-black living room. I feel with my fingers down the hallway to the bedrooms. Michael's bedroom. Then the one I shared with him back when we still had Ben. I lie on the floor where my bed would have been. I turn off an imaginary lamp, pull up an imaginary blanket, imagine I am sleeping.

I let memories fill up my head for a while. Me and Michael at four and fourteen, playing flashlight tag. He was always a good big brother, even when he was a kid. Me and Michael at ten and twenty, staying up to set off fireworks at midnight on New Year's.

Me and Michael at five and fifteen, sitting down at the kitchen table for a serious talk with Ben. Noticing he was the only parent in the room.

Me and Michael at eight and eighteen, cleaning the house, waiting for word.

I have to think about breathing. In-in-in. Out slow. But it doesn't seem to work this time, and tears well up from somewhere. I want to scream and sob and break things, but all that happens is, I lie perfectly still and tears drip down the sides of my face into my hair. The night passes one wide-awake minute at a time.

I guess I fall asleep around dawn. I know because when I wake, it's completely daylight, and I can see that the apartment walls are not the right color. There is a ladder in the corner, near the front door. There are drop cloths. There are paint cans.

I scurry out. I feel desperate, like I'm late for something. I run. I need to reach home before anybody realizes I'm gone. But I know it's too late for that; the sun's already up. I feel a stab of guilt, adding to the missing persons list in the Harless household. I run faster. I trip. I'm never as fast as I need to be.

Bloody knees and scratched-up palms are the first things to reach Hubert's door. He flings it open as I get there. He has the phone in his hand, says into it, "Never mind, she's home." He is red from head to toe; even his shirt is red. His hand on my elbow is rough.

"What the hell was you thinking?"

I've never heard his voice like this. The last voice I heard like this was Ben's. Michael never raised his voice or grabbed me this way. I scramble backward, wrench free from Hubert's grip. He follows, and I can feel his footsteps shaking the porch. We will have to spend some time this summer firming it up with wooden joists, knocking in nails till it can weather storms like this.

"Dang it, Sasha!"

I trip down the stairs. I spin in the dirt and run. My heart has gone ahead of my brain. In my brain, everything is calm and slow. But my heart pounds. My hands shake.

I have one foot on the road when Hubert gets hold of me again. He pulls me back by my shirt, and I almost fall. A noise escapes me, something like the noise Michael made when they told us Ben was dead. Hubert lets go of me and balls his fists against his pockets for a second. Then he turns around and starts beating the hell out of his pickup truck, cursing and kicking till the door dents in. Curses spill out of him. I stand a few feet away, wishing I could run. My feet feel like they've grown roots. My brain has caught up and now my heart feels too slow.

Hubert stops beating up the truck and stands still except for his shoulders, which go up and down. His face is violet, but it's starting to fade back to red. There's blood on his knuckles, and I hand him a rag out of the back of the truck.

Hubert won't look at me. He reaches for me and I tense, but this time he means to hug me. He squeezes me to him. I can smell his sweat and feel his muscles. After a minute he lets me go. He walks toward the porch without saying a word or waiting for me to follow.

We don't look for Mikey the next day, or the next day. Each day I expect that we will, and then the sun rises, and then it walks across the sky, and then it sinks, and we still haven't managed to get out of the house. Hubert has all but stopped going to the mines. I don't even know if he still has a job. He doesn't speak except to Marla and Sara, who are louder than usual, picking up on all the stress. They're in trouble all the time with Shirley. Hubert is too clean to be Hubert. He walks out to the shed after dinner. I stand at the door and watch him organize and reorganize the boxes. To my horror, he stops and hides his face in his hands for a while, and his shoulders shake. I turn away quickly.

Inside, Shirley's got the TV on. Since Dogwood, the old arguments have flared up again on the local news: Is coal worth the cost? Is there a better source of energy? Are the jobs worth it when our miners aren't safe?

But nobody in this town is safe. Doesn't matter if you mine coal or don't. You can fight a fire. You can be nine years old. I think about my last words to Michael and how they were probably "Later!" or "After a while!" I think about telling Mikey, "I'll catch up!" Before Ben left for his night shift, and when Judy put me to bed, I probably told each of them I'd see them in the morning. None of those things turned out to be true.

When Hubert says good night that evening, I don't say it back.

part three

1. Haiku

Write five syllables.
Then write seven syllables.
Then you write five more.

—SENT JUNE 24

POETRY NEWSLETTER

I print the first one
and I tape it in my book.
I don't email back.

ONE

I had a friend once.
We spent our days on the porch.
Now I'm alone here.

QUIET

I do not talk now.
I do not talk to people.
I do not have words.

IF

If Ben and Judy
were here right now, I would not
say a word to them.

THE MISSING MINERS

Shirley's TV says
they're still looking for bodies.
Oh God, I forgot.

IN OTHER NEWS

Shirley's TV says
they're still looking for Mikey.
It's coming Week Five.

AND NOW FOR THE WEATHER

Shirley's TV says
it's the perfect summer day.
Enjoy yourself, folks!

2. Quatrain

Write one line.
Then three others.
It doesn't have to rhyme,
so this one doesn't.

—SENT JULY 1

THE DAY THEY FIND THE MINERS

All the major stations show
the weeping and the flowers.
Then the weatherman arrives
to speak of summer showers.

"FILL THE MINER'S HAT" DONATION STATION

Signs go up at Save-Great:
"If you can, please give!"
I don't know who the money's for.
Nobody lived.

232

MIKEY

We do look for him, but we don't feel
like we will ever find him. Still,
this is not something we say out loud.
We keep silent. That's our deal.

FUNERALS

Hubert doesn't go to work
and he doesn't go pay his respects.
Shirley nags and nags at him.
I don't know what she expects.

SUMMERS PAST

This time last year, I dozed upside down
    on the couch
with my feet on the wall and my head
    on the floor.
Summer day after summer day dripped by
    like lemonade.
I complained and complained, "Michael,
    I'm bored!"

I'M GLAD IT'S SUMMER

Who could sit at a desk on a day like this?
Who could focus on pages through this beam
    of sun?
Full of anger, hope, and fear,
I am faced with a choice: hold fast or run?

ELSEWHERE

This road in front of Hubert's house,
empty in the evening light,
leads to a two-lane that leads to a highway,
goes places I've never seen, but might.

CAUGHT

Lights flash,
sirens bleat,
I get caught
on Main Street.

CLOSE SUPERVISION

Hubert and Shirley
come out of their haze.
They watch me closer
for all of three days.

3. Cinquain

Noun.

Adjective, adjective.

Three-word verb.

Four words about feelings.

Synonym.

—SENT JULY 8

Sasha.
She's lost.
She walks along,
looking up at clouds,
quiet.

Anger,
pointless, nauseous,
waits in shadow
like an evil spirit.
Always.

WHAT FAMILY DOES

Leave.
They do.
They all do.
That's what I know
now.

MIKEY

Kid,
lost, alone,
went somewhere else.
Hope we find him
soon.

4. Epistle

Dear Poet,

In an epistle

you write a letter

to someone. You don't have to follow

rules of syllable, meter, rhyme,

or rhythm, but it shouldn't

necessarily

sound like crap, either.

—SENT JULY 15

Dear Judy,

I walked to the Burger Bargain today.

The whole place smelled like onions.

The ladies there can cut onions without
        crying,

knives slashing down, whacking on the

chopped-up cutting board.

Bam! Like a baby falling from her chair.

Wham! Like a car door slamming.

I sort of wonder if

the day you figured out you were able

to slice into onions without crying

was the day you decided
it was okay
to leave.

Dear Ben,
I remember the little things
about you, like your dirty fingernails,
your card games on the coffee table,
the way you spread your dinner to the
edges of your plate to make it look
like you took more when you really
left the most for us.
I've forgotten other things about you,
like the words you choose, and if you like
    poems,
and the meter and rhyme and rhythm
of your voice.

Dear Mikey,
I guess I sort of understand why
you haven't come back yet.
If I had me for a cousin,
I might not think about
coming back, either.

Still.
Maybe you'll change your mind someday?
Maybe you'll change your mind today?

Dear City Planners,
I don't get
why you picked
this exact rock
in this exact valley.
Had a squirrel already claimed
all the other rocks
in all the other valleys?

Dear Dr. Shaw,
Mr. Powell swears
you know your stuff,
even though you give names
to things that should have
other names.
You call it "depression."
You call it "anxiety."
I call it "Look what happened."
I call it "Everybody leaves."

You send me home
with orange bottles
that rattle in the console
of Hubert's old truck
on the quiet, quiet, quiet
ride back.
This medicine
is not going to help
unless it can bring back
the missing
and what Pastor Ramey calls
the "gone home."

Dear Michael,

Dear Shirley,
I wish you would lay off
the stupid apples already.
Also, why must you
stomp through the living room
at six thirty a.m. on a Saturday?
Can't you tell I'm sleeping?

Dear Michael,

Dear Anthony,
It was nice the way
you started to walk over to me
on the final day of school
like you wanted to say something.
It was nice, too, that you stopped
and turned away.
I might have cried.
I might have spoken.
See you in August.

Dear Michael.

5. Enclosed Tercet

A tercet is three lines.
When you write it in enclosed form,
the first and the last lines rhyme.

—SENT JULY 22

ONLINE

Shirley sits on her blue chair,
but she doesn't notice who's around her,
nor does she care.

FRAGILE

There is peace in this dwelling
as long as we don't discuss Mikey.
If we do, there is yelling.

HOW JULY FELT

Bug-loud days
loomed wide open, filled me with panic.
I'm not okay.

IF I DON'T WRITE

The line between calm and not gets blurry.
I shake and get lost in my head.
I breathe quick and I worry.

MAKING HUBERT MAD

I stayed at the grocery store too long.
Hubert thought I was someplace else,
but he was wrong.

THIS PLACE

Michael wanted to leave so bad
that staying never felt possible.
I wonder how I'd feel if it had.

6. Found Poetry

On a website,
I found this:
a found poem
is a poem you discover
in your environment
that nobody else
realized
was poetry.

—SENT JULY 29

GRACE DANIELS,

wife of miner Barry Daniels,
waits with other family members
outside a southern West Virginia
elementary school.

NOT

intended as a substitute
for medical care. Consult
a physician if symptoms
persist.

FOUNDED

by Hat Casswell
in 1843, the town
of Caboose predates
the state of West
Virginia.

MISSING

since May.
Last seen in
Alley Rush
wearing
blue T-shirt

and stonewashed
(nuh-uh, just faded)
jeans
(and an innocent face).

START OF AUGUST

with
record highs
        (and new lows)

7. Tanka

First, write a haiku.
Five syllables, seven, five.
Then you add some more:
one seven-syllable line,
two seven-syllable lines.

—SENT AUGUST 5

PHYLLIS

Says she'll still love me
even when the other kid
comes to stay next month.
I have no rights to Phyllis,
so I don't know why I'm sad.

UNSAID

There are many rules
to writing good poetry.
I don't always know
how to fit inside those rules.
Sometimes things get left unsaid.

MICHAEL

Why do all the things
I write come back to Michael?
Why do all the things
I write come back to Michael?
There is no one named Michael.

8. Triplets

Triplets are poems
made of three lines.
Usually they rhyme.

—SENT AUGUST 12

HARLESS HOUSEHOLD

Nobody is sleeping.
Most of us are weeping.
There are secrets not worth keeping.

NIGHT FIGHTS

Hubert and Shirley scream and howl,
yell some words that are very foul,
then one or the other throws in the towel.

FALLING APART

Hubert finally goes back to work.
The girls are bouncing off the walls, berserk.
Even Shirley's lost her smirk.

AUGUST

Summer waves the edges
of Phyllis's trimmed hedges.
We're all balanced on ledges.

MIKEY

I miss baking muffins and playing with the
    dog.
I can't think clearly with him gone.
I am lost in a fog.

MICHAEL

When I think of my older brother
dying of smoke inhalation,
I can't breathe and I can't rhyme.

BACK TO SCHOOL

For the first two days, everyone is thrilled
to see each other as the doors are sealed.
Even in the warm air, I feel chilled.

9. Poems That Tell a Story

Let me tell you a story.
Once upon a time, a handsome,
dashing young poet
sent out the final newsletter
as a welcome back to school present
and as a reminder that if
you're entering the August contest
(AND YOU ARE),
you need to bring me a poem
by the end of the week.
And they lived happily ever after.
The End

—SENT AUGUST 19

WHAT I DID

on my summer vacation
by sasha harless
i forgot how to use
the following things
punctuation
capitalization
and the sound
of my voice
i forgot how to
cook muffins
i forgot how to babysit
and how to clean out sheds
and how to save money for guitars
and i forgot again and again
which house i live in

THERE IS A NEW KID

next door, and she is
Mikey's age, and she is
beautiful, with
calm, combed hair
and sweet, dimpled cheeks
and, as far as I can tell,
normal eating habits.
Phyllis shines with love.
The two of them invite me over,
but I shake my head and stay on Hubert's
    front porch,
alone except for his work boots.

ASSIGNMENT

Now that school's in
and I still won't talk,
Mr. Powell asks me to
write something down,
and my new English teacher
asks me to write something down.
Mr. Powell wants my goals for the year.
Mr. Hart wants my goals for English class,
and what I think a fair grading system would
   be,
and what I hope to learn and accomplish.
It seems like a lot of faith to put
in a silent eighth grader.
Isn't he the one
who went to college
for this?

THE STORY OF MY LIFE

This is the assignment
for the second week of school:
we are required to write our history,
the story of our lives. I watch
my classmates folded over their notebooks.
I watch pencils scratch. I watch heads get
   scratched.
This boy in black, he is looking at the ceiling
and smiling
as if there is a great secret written there.
I think his life has been interesting.
I think I would like to read his story.
The girls in the corner
look lost. You can't understand
what makes a good story
if you've never starred in one,
or at least been a particularly memorable
(sometimes tragic)
supporting character.

INTERVENTION

At least that's what it feels like
the day Jaina and Anthony corner me
by the lockers in the English wing.
"We're worried about you, Sasha."
"You still haven't given me a poem for the
    contest.
We all lost the one in May. We've got to
kick butt in the August round!"
"Right . . ." Jaina looks at him
like he's grown another head.
"And also, you don't talk anymore."
They maybe should have planned
their intervention a little better.
I don't say anything,
and Jaina shrugs, and walks slowly away.
"I'm here if you need me,"
she says as she goes,
but she gets farther away as she says it.
When she's gone, Anthony waits
and does this half smile, like he already knows
what I'm about to hand him.
He gives my notebook back after class the
    next day,
with a note written on the first blank page:

Unless you stop me, I'm sending three of these
    to the contest.
Please don't stop me.
I'm glad it's still you in there.

10. FREE VERSE AND MIXED FORMS

Now that summer's over,
there's no newsletter to help.
I have to figure out for myself
how to say what needs to be said.
—STARTED AUGUST 26

ON WEEKENDS

We look for two Michael Harlesses
on the streets of Beckley
(the kids throwing Frisbees,
and popping balloons,
and chasing each other,
splashing through the fountain).
We look for Mikey and we look—
I look
for my Michael,
who can't possibly have left me
this alone
for this long.

POINTLESS?

Search
without end.
Kicking through stones,
peering into every face.
Failing.

THERE IS A COLLEGE CAMPUS HERE

And I dream of graduating
and I dream of seeing Mikey graduate
and I dream of both of us living life happy,
free of our sad past.
Today is not that day.
Today I hang flier after flier after flier
on power poles.

AUTHORITIES

They say they have not given up on him,
but every week the spotlight continues to dim,
and hope spreads thin.

WHAT I HEARD SOMEONE SAY

"Poor folks,
thinking that kid
will ever come back.
That kid is dead, man."

SECRET

I am secretly a bad person.
I am secretly a bad cousin.
I am secretly awful.
Let me tell you why.
I have come
to expect, to rely on,
to enjoy,
our trips up
Beckley way.

STEPS OF THE BECKLEY COURTHOUSE

I sit and wait to be picked up.
Hubert is checking on some things
he doesn't want me to hear.
There are fluffy springtime clouds
in the late summer sky,
and kids shuffle by
like they have all the
time in the world.
A kid about fifteen or sixteen
walks from the Go-Mart with a
Snickers bar and a Coke.
One bite gone. Then, later,
a sip. Like the treat
and the perfect afternoon
will last forever.

11. HAIKU ONCE MORE

I have been too wild.
I will rein in my poems.
I will write haiku.
    —SEPTEMBER 2

des today.
nt of truth
e.

ot

11. HAIKU ONCE MORE

I have been too wild.
I will rein in my poems.
I will write haiku.
—SEPTEMBER 2

NOT ME

We got grades today.
It is the moment of truth
for people who care.

C-MINUS

I was supposed to
write about my own life, not
other people's lives.

NOTES

Jaina passes one
to Lisa and Lisa laughs
and writes her one back.

TODAY

Windowpanes rattled
with anger and thunder when
the sun went away.

JAINA'S QUESTION

"Sasha, why don't you
talk no more?" she asks again.
Wish I could tell her.

12. CINQUAIN ONCE MORE

This
is the
worst day I've
had in a long
time.

Darkness
is everywhere.
In the sky.
Here in my head.
Midnight.

Home
was Mikey.
Home was Phyllis;
was Ben, Judy, and
Michael.

Teacher
in math
thinks I'm stupid.
She tells me she
cares.

Rules
of poetry
insist I shouldn't
break the cinquain pattern.
Who the hell says?

Panic
is sneaky.
Creeps up slowly
like a hunting cat.
Pounces.

13. TANKAS ONCE MORE

—SEPTEMBER 16

VISITORS

A knock at the door!
Sometimes the police visit
to keep us informed.
Sometimes it's Pastor Ramey,
who brings toys for my cousins.

SCHOOL HALLS

Anthony walks me
from English to my locker
in total silence.
"You okay?" he asks at last.
I nod a quick lie at him.

SCHOOL HALLS (PART TWO)

Jaina walks with me
from Spanish to my locker,
nervously speaking.
She tries to fill the quiet,
but does not know what to say.

SCHOOL HALLS (PART THREE)

I walk my own self
from my locker to the bus,
my head full of words.
They rattle around in there,
but they refuse to shake loose.

14. ENCLOSED TERCET ONCE MORE

How many lines? Write three.
The middle is different. It doesn't rhyme.
The middle one is me.
—SEPTEMBER 23

THE ORANGE BOTTLE

It's for anxiety. I'm supposed to take it every
   day.
It makes my mouth dry and my head ache.
I still don't have anything to say.

WHAT THEY MEAN BY "ANXIETY"

is that sometimes the classroom gets too loud
and I'm afraid Mikey will call for me and I
   won't hear him,
so I get up and leave, and that's not allowed.

THE POLICE COME AGAIN

On foot, I leave school, a place I'd rather avoid.
It's dark outside and in the house when I get
    home.
The police should be worried, but instead
    they're annoyed.

SHIRLEY'S PUNISHMENT

"We tried being nice so's you wouldn't go
    roam.
We had the patience of Job, but the Good Lord
    knows that didn't work.
You're grounded from writing them poems."

need

too

see   too   dark to

write but

this way

won't catch me

THE POLICE COME AGAIN

On foot, I leave school, a place I'd rathe
It's dark outside and in the house wh
home.
The police should be worried, but
they're annoyed.

SHIRLEY'S PUNISHMENT

"We tried being nice so's you wou
roam.
We had the patience of Job, but th
knows that didn't work.
You're grounded from writing t

I   need
my
words
It is too
dark to   see   too   dark to
        write but
                this way
shirley won't catch me

riting.

to be

my name.
et have other names.

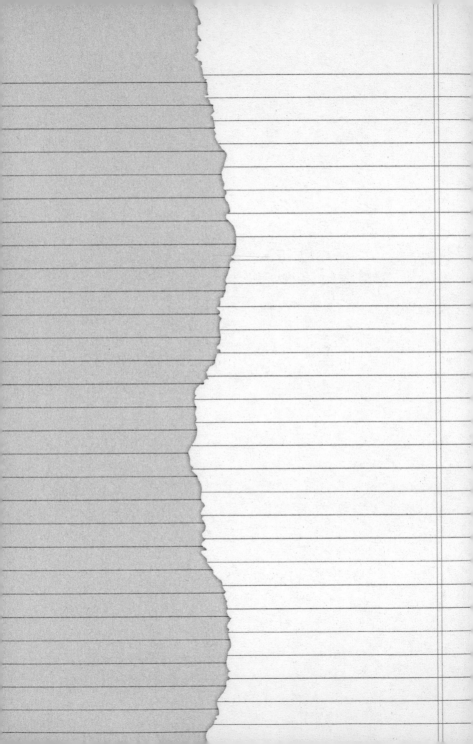

IN TROUBLE

Days and days, I walk,
not talking and not writing.
I am a shadow.

SHIRLEY

I think she thinks she's
helping when she tries to be
strict like a parent.

CRAZY

Yesterday I thought
about following in the
footsteps of Aster.
The orange bottle has my name.
The ones in the cabinet have other names.

OCTOBER 2

Grounding
is supposed
to be a
week, but Hubert takes
pity.

SAVED

Hubert makes Shirley let me off the hook.
I'm glad. It's time for poetry club.
I'm going to need my notebook.

RELIEF

I'm relieved to have my notebook.
I'm relieved to have my pen.
I'm relieved that when I have a thought
I can write it down again.

ANTHONY TRIES

And tries and tries and tries
to get some words out of me.
I try, too, but they will not rise
from down in the depths of me.

MY SCHEDULE

Work around the house
with Hubert on Mondays
Mr. Powell on Tuesdays
Beckley for therapy Wednesdays
Thursdays are poetry club
Fridays I work at the pawnshop
to replace the window
I don't remember
breaking while
I was barred
from writing
poetry.

SPY IN THE GRASS

Hubert says,
"We're treading water, Phyllis.
She's working off the window uptown,
and the only reason they didn't suspend her
for leaving school that day is she's . . .
special.
That's what they're calling her.
Special.
She's taking them dang pills
that are supposed to calm her down
and I don't see them making a
danged bit of difference
and she still ain't spoke a
word."
There is silence while, I'm sure, Phyllis is
patting Hubert's hand or
squeezing his shoulder.
I scratch at the window frame
and rotted wood comes off under my
   fingernails.
Underneath are termites.
"Keep treading," Phyllis says.
"That little girl needs us

to keep her head above water."
Then I am deeply embarrassed
and deeply grateful
and I stop listening at the window
and follow Stella through the grass.

OCTOBER 8

Today is Mikey's tenth birthday.
I want to bake muffins.
But the pilot light
won't stay lit
and then there is a
sopping mess of batter on the stove
and a sobbing mess of girl on the floor.

I HAVE STOPPED

corralling
my poems
by form.
They run
loose like
wild dogs.

SIX DAYS OF BEING LEFT IN PEACE
TO MOURN MIKEY

Shirley takes the babies
and goes to stay
with her mother
for six days.
When she comes home,
I am lying on the couch
watching the fruit flies
circle the broken ceiling fan.
She shakes her head
and walks into the kitchen,
where she throws out the black bananas
and the green wheat bread.

She has to see the tears rolling
sideways into my hair, and how Hubert
will not hold his head up, but she
does not ask us if we are okay.
She pushes back the curtains
and opens the window
to dump the moldy coffee,
six days old, from the pot.
She mutters under her breath,
"This is a shame,
is what this is."

15. EPISTLE REVISITED

—OCTOBER 19

Dear Michael,

You don't know the other Michael Harless,
but he's ten.
He has light brown hair
and light green eyes
and I've only ever seen his face clean once.
He has a different first name,
but he's a Michael Harless
and he does things like he doggone means
    them.

I wonder if you could keep an eye out for him.
If you could just check and make sure he's
    all right.
I know you wanted me to get out of Caboose,
and I thought that's what I wanted, too,
but for right now, I need Mikey to come home
    with me
and let us finish growing up before we choose.
I don't want to let you down.

But Mikey's ten
and his name is Michael Harless
and I don't want him to die.

Can you find him for me?

Dear Mikey,
I've spent a lot of time wishing that we never
    opened the box.
That we never walked in the sun, ate
    strawberries from the fields,
slept in a meadow under the stars, bought
    hot dogs from a street vendor,
and ran from the police.

But all those things happened.
And there are other things that happened.
Your mother loved you enough to take you
    with her when she left.
Your father loved you enough to come and
    find you.

Your cousin loved you enough to take you away
    so you didn't get hurt.
I've been mad at you for not coming home
    when all those people love you,
but I guess what we love is that you do things
    your own way.
And sometimes I want just one person
to love that about me.

I'm not mad anymore.
If you come back,
I will make you a dozen gnarled finger-bone
    muffins with extra chocolate
and we'll lie on the front porch in the sun
and you won't have to tell me where
    you've been
if you don't want to.

And if you don't come back,
I'll think about you all the time,
and when I travel someday,
I'll keep an eye out for you.

But I finally get it.
You've got to decide for yourself
Where you want to be.

SPEAK

Once,
there was the crackle of a radio
and a voice calling for Michael Harless,
who was never going to answer.
His silence sank into my heart slowly,
but it did sink.

Tonight,
There is the ringing of a phone,
And the voice of Mikey Harless
Begs to come home.
The line, once silent, comes alive.
Two voices get found.

part four

26

"Do you think he's mad at me?"

Hubert about drives the truck off the road when I speak, halfway up to Beckley in the middle of the night. It's not the first time tonight that I've done it—I told him Mikey was on the phone—but I guess after five months of quiet, he's not used to the sound of my voice.

"Sasha, Mikey gets mad for no reason sometimes. I don't want you to worry that you've done something wrong."

"Well, did he sound mad to you? He sounded mad to me. And I *did* do something wrong."

"Nobody's mad at you," Hubert promises. Which doesn't mean the same thing as telling me I didn't do anything wrong.

I can't sit still. I tug at the seat belt, tuck my feet up under me, let them down again. The drive to Beckley's gotten familiar, but this midnight trip feels more like when me and Mikey ran away than a normal drive.

Hubert's got directions written down on the top page of Shirley's apple-shaped notepad. He looks at them so often, I'm afraid he's not looking at the road enough, but before long, he's got us steered out the other side of town and down a road that winds next to a creek.

"Is he living out here?" I ask. I haven't seen any houses in a while.

"I don't know," he says. "He just put her on the phone, and she gave me directions."

"You talked to Mikey's mom?"

"Enough to get directions."

"Well, how'd . . . how'd she sound?" It feels strange to be talking, but I can't keep all the questions in. My heart hammers in my chest, and I curl and uncurl my fingers. What if something happens and Mikey's not where Aster said he'd be?

Hubert wipes a hand quickly down his face, and I feel the truck speed up. I think Hubert must feel the same way I do, like we need to get there as fast as we can.

"She sounded like Aster," he answered, in a voice that implies that's not a good thing.

I'm expecting Mikey—filthy face, tough-guy attitude—but what we see when we pull up to the long stone building is a blanket-wrapped bundle in a stranger's arms. At least to me she's a stranger. I know who she is, though; would know even if we hadn't talked about her. Aster looks just like Mikey. Same light brown hair, same narrowed eyes.

We've met at what Mikey called "home," a run-down old train station, red cinder block next to rusted lengths of unused track. The broken windows look like something I might have done on a bad day, which frightens me. I don't want to think I have anything in common with this woman who got addicted, who lives in a train station, and who kept a lost boy.

Aster looks almost sweet as she presses the bundle of blankets into Hubert's arms. She's wearing shorts even though it's the first of November, and her eyes look old. She never seems to look directly at anybody, not even Hubert, who she used to love so much she married him. I'm not sure she even knows I'm here. I watch her eyes move from Mikey's hair to the quilt to the hood of the truck and back again. I watch Hubert, how he can't take his eyes off her.

"Aster," he says. "It's cold outside. Why don't you come home with us?"

I imagine what that might look like, introducing Aster to Shirley. But Aster shakes her head, pressing on the lump of blankets that is her son. "No, I'm good, I'm good here. I'll stay here. You take the boy, Hubert. You take our boy, you take him now." She keeps saying these words over and over, pressing on Hubert's arms, pressing us toward the truck, pressing the door closed behind us. Through the window, she keeps saying it. "You take good care of our boy, Hubert Harless. You take care of him." She has a necklace of a heart, and the cheap metal's left a green stripe around her neck. Her hands shake as she reaches into the blankets, stroking Mikey's hair.

Mikey doesn't wake up or look back as the truck reverses onto vine-covered pavement that's too old to be sturdy enough anymore for cars. We rumble over rocks and chunks of old gravel as we pull away. Me and Hubert have Mikey propped between us, heavy head bouncing from my shoulder to his. In the side view I can see his mother's hair as she leans into the wind. I know it's impossible, but I think I can see her dry, cold cheeks. She's holding her last blanket closed with her hands. I think about what it must have meant to her to give up two of her blankets to Mikey, leaving him wrapped as she handed him to us. I think of what it must have taken, of how much of a mother she must still be, to hand him to us. I shiver in the full-blast heat from the vent.

Mikey sleeps all the way to the hospital. He stretches at one point, and his legs fall across me, toes curling against the door handle. His skin is filthy and warm. A couple of times he moves, and I know he's trying not to wake up, trying not to face us or anything else just yet. I know he'll be quiet for a while. I might have to talk for both of us.

In the light of a passing car, I see tears on Hubert's face.

They're rolling silently down into his beard. I think about the woman in the abandoned train station, in shorts and a sweater, clutching her quilt. I think about how he used to love her. I think about the look she had on her face when we drove away. She looked like Michael when we got the news about Ben. Like Phyllis when I broke her GUI-tar. Helpless. Like we'd pulled the cord on the last light in her life.

Hubert wakes Mikey at the hospital. It takes him a minute to blink awake, but once he does, he flings himself at Hubert, winding skinny arms around his neck.

"Hey. Hey there, buddy. Okay." Hubert keeps him wrapped in the blankets and carries him inside. I think about the first time I ran away from Phyllis and how they gave me an IV and took care of my feet. I don't know what might be wrong with Mikey, and I'm not sure whether I'm supposed to talk to him. I decide not to talk unless he talks first.

I'm asleep in the waiting room when Hubert comes to find me a while later. "We can go," he says softly. He's got Mikey in his arms, now wrapped in a clean blanket and sound asleep again.

At home, Hubert carries Mikey past Shirley's car, which is parked at the edge of the driveway with the motor running. He takes Mikey into the house and tucks him into his bed. He comes back out to deal with Shirley, who is following two steps behind him.

"He's okay?" she asks.

"He's okay. Lost some weight. A little dehydrated. But he's okay."

"Oh, I'm so glad, Hugh. I'm so glad he's home," she says. The sound of her voice is so odd that I look up to study her face. Her eyes are shining with tears, and she reaches up to touch Hubert's cheek. "I knew you'd bring him home."

"Shirley, why's your car running?"

She turns away, walks into the girls' room, and comes back a minute later with a sleeping Sara in her arms. "We're going to be at my mother's if you need us."

"Shirl?"

"I couldn't leave a man who had lost his son," Shirley says. "You've got your boy back. Now I can go."

The words take a minute to sink in, and then I feel the breath punch out of me. *Poor Hubert!* I think.

"But . . . my girls . . ." He reaches a hand toward Sara, tucks a loose curl behind her ear.

Shirley watches him do it. "You'll see them. I'm not going to keep you from them." Her breath hitches and she passes him, carrying Sara out the front door to the waiting car. When she returns a moment later, Hubert has already picked up Marla and is cradling her under his chin. Shirley takes the sleeping girl from him, kisses her hair, and heads for the door. I reach out to touch a bit of Marla's hair as Shirley carries her by. Hubert and I follow them to the porch, and she comes back to face him, standing on the bottom porch step like she wants to climb back up, but thinks better of it.

"Please don't do this," he says. His voice sounds so rough that I'm afraid he might be crying. "Shirl, I love you. Please don't go."

"Aww, Hubert . . ." She lays her fingertips against his forehead. "I know that right *here*, you think you love me." Then she moves her palm to cover his heart. "But I haven't been right *here* in too long, and, honey, that's where I'd need to be if it was ever going to work." It's the sweetest and the calmest I've ever heard her voice sound, even though her face is tearstained. She kisses Hubert once on his scraggly cheek and walks back to the car, climbs behind the wheel. She backs up quickly enough that the tailpipe scrapes the embankment on the other side of the road. She pulls out, first onto gravel, then onto pavement. Leaves rustle back and forth in front of the taillights, making them flicker. It's hard to tell when the exact last moment is that we can still see them.

Hubert sits for a long while, reading to Mikey even though he's asleep. Then staring at him and staring at him. I watch from the couch, peeking through the crack in the bedroom door. When Hubert falls asleep there on the floor, Mikey crawls out of bed and comes into the living room, trailing a quilt. He crawls onto the couch beside me. He curls up with his head on my shoulder. He sleeps after a while. He still hasn't spoken.

I stay awake.

Which is good, because it takes three hours to get the house clean. Dust is swept out into the dark yard. Long-neglected corners are mopped as dawn is breaking, left to dry in the sun with the windows open. The cold autumn morning plays with the curtains and sprinkles leaves onto the rug.

There are things I can't fix and things I can. I can get the stains off the molding. I kneel with a dish sponge, inching around the length of the kitchen, then the living room, then Mikey's room, then Hubert's. I leave the bathroom till last, because the black mold has begun to grow up the shower and I don't want to ruin the sponge until I'm finished with it. The sun hitches higher. I scrub and scrub.

When ten o'clock rolls around and Mikey and Hubert are both still asleep, I turn on the TV to Saturday infomercials, the way Shirley would have done by now. I raise the volume, but nobody stirs. So I put my shoulder into the black mold and I toss the old sponge and I scrub-scrub-scrub with Shirley's left-behind toothbrush. After a while, the bathroom tiles sparkle. They are paler blue than I thought. I take the rugs out onto the porch and shake them. Phyllis is out there with her new girl. They're both bundled up, tossing a stick for Chip to fetch.

"Phyllis."

Her head whips around sharply. "Lord above!" she exclaims. "Have I missed that voice!" She crosses to me and wraps me tightly in a hug. The girl drifts along behind her, looking lost.

I wrap my arms around Phyllis, and I don't let go when I say, "He's home."

She moves quickly to hold me at arm's length. "Mikey?" When I nod, her eyes fill up."He's okay. He's still sleeping, but he's okay."

"Well." She wrings her hands, smooths my hair and then her new borrowed kid's "Well. Miss Phoebe, I think this calls for a very special dessert. Will you help me in the kitchen?"

The little girl nods shyly.

"Miss Sasha, would you care to join us?"

"I'm going to stay here," I tell her. I can't help but be a little jealous, with Phoebe getting Phyllis's attention, but it's more than that. "I want to be here when he wakes up."

Mikey wakes before Hubert, at a little past one in the afternoon. I've tried to make breakfast, and mangled it. The biscuits are hard as stones. The gravy is too thin. I was probably supposed to grease a pan or something. I toss breakfast in the trash and sit next to Mikey while he finishes waking.

"Hey," he says.

Mikey was only quiet for a single night, and I'm relieved

to hear his voice. I think of how Hubert and Phyllis must feel, hearing my voice after months of quiet. Mikey sounds older than he used to, and he's gotten taller. His hair, once spiky, has grown out past his ears and lies in soft, light brown tangles. He's thinner and his eyes are set deeper in his lean face.

"Hey," I answer.

I don't know why, maybe because I haven't heard his voice in so many months, maybe because I've barely heard my own voice in as many months, but all of a sudden I'm swallowed up by tears that need to fall, and sobs that need to whoop out before they crack my chest from the inside. I bolt off the couch and into the kitchen. I throw the skillet onto the stove again, determined to get these biscuits right.

Mikey and me and Hubert sit on Phyllis's porch with the plate of muffins she and Phoebe have made for us. Chip and Stella are in the yard, picking over the ruined biscuits and gravy.

"I'll teach you," Phyllis tells me every time my breath hitches from crying. I nod, even though I'm not crying about the stupid biscuits.

Mikey has eaten three muffins. The rest of us take one apiece, except for Hubert, who doesn't take any. We wait to see how many Mikey will want. He starts on a fourth. Though he's had a long bath today, he's still hiding under a layer of grime. He stops halfway through the fourth muffin and starts looking green around the edges.

"Slow down, Mikey," Phyllis says.

He does, and now that his mouth isn't full, we're all waiting. He must know it, but he doesn't start talking for the longest time, and I can relate.

Mikey is not very good at telling us the story. When I ask him how he survived alone, he says, "I thought about what you would do, Sash. And then I did that."

"Oh, holy crap. It's a miracle you survived."

It takes him three days to get the whole story out. The police come, and talk to Mikey, and piece a few things together, but some things we still don't know. Like how he survived the first week down in Alley Rush, before he caught a ride to Beckley and escaped outside the police station. We know he lived in someone's outbuilding, but we can't imagine what he ate or what he drank or how he stayed calm. I think about what I would have done, like Mikey said, and I don't know.

"I ate from the farmer's market," he says. "I stole stuff. I figured you'd say it was okay to steal stuff just for that week."

I squeeze him. "I would have said that," I promise.

He tells us that once he got to Beckley, he got adopted by a man living out on the street.

"A vagrant," the police say.

"Gary," is what Mikey says.

Gary taught Mikey how to find food, and shelter, and sometimes money.

"Found dead of advanced cirrhosis of the liver," the police say.

"Gary didn't come back one night," is what Mikey says.

But Gary had taught Mikey well. So Mikey went out to find shelter on his own. He found it in an abandoned red train station far outside of town. He lived there alone for two long, scary nights, with, he swears, the sound of ghost trains. Then somebody else joined him there.

Having seen his face on all the telephone poles, Mikey's mother went out looking for him. At the same time we were on the street asking bored college people, she was looking in empty buildings and safe hiding places. She knew all the places a homeless child might sleep. She found him in the train station, and they set up house, the two of them together.

"Family," Mikey says. "Except she kept taking off."

"For how long?" Hubert asks, his voice pitched low and sad.

"A couple days. And she'd come back different."

"At least she didn't do that part in front of you," Hubert says, and I realize where she went when she disappeared.

"It got cold," Mikey said. "I wanted us to find a house, but she didn't care about that. So I called home." His eyes travel from my face to his father's, and his voice chokes up. "I thought it would be Shirley to answer. I didn't know either one of you would be here."

"I know, buddy." Hubert eases closer, wrapping an arm around his son's shoulders. I want to say I'm sorry for making him think the worst about his dad, but the words get stuck in my throat.

He isn't crying, which amazes me, but his voice, when he says the last part, gets so small. "I thought she'd come with me."

Hubert pulls him roughly into a one-armed hug. "She wanted to," he says. "She *wants* to. She's just . . . it's an illness, Mikey. An illness she's been fighting for a long time."

The whole story ought to be written down. But I haven't touched my notebook in days.

27

Me and Hubert work on the porch.
Then on the windows. Instead of putting up plastic, we
put in new glass. The wind stays out as November drops
the temperatures.

Mikey works, too. His hands have gotten steadier. He
works like he's so much older than ten. On the coldest
nights, he thinks of his mother. I know because those are
the nights he doesn't sleep. He's like he used to be, quiet
and wide awake. He sits up on the far end of the couch,
and I stay on my end, but I keep a blanket around him.
I never know what to say. He chews his fingers and he
watches late-night movies that I shouldn't let him watch.
I turn down the movies at the worst parts, but I leave the
TV on for light.

At dawn, after Hubert leaves for work, Mikey falls

asleep on the couch with his legs hanging off the edge. I think of a day a hundred years ago, Mikey asleep on the rug with an arm over Chip. I think we should be next door cooking muffins with Phyllis. But those days feel like something I dreamed. I don't sit on her front porch at four a.m. anymore, though sometimes she still slips me an egg salad sandwich across the fence. I built the fence, with Hubert. Mikey followed behind us, holding the nails between his lips.

I stay home for a couple of days with Mikey before Hubert says we both have to go back to school. Phoebe and Mikey climb onto the bus to the elementary school, and I wait for the middle school bus.

Jaina's sitting with some new friends, but she raises her chin at me when I get on the bus.

"I heard your cousin came back," she says.

I smile a little, but I don't know what to say. I shuffle my way to an empty seat as the bus starts moving again.

Anthony is waiting at my locker. "Sasha! I heard there's good news!"

I nod.

"Well? How is he? Is he all right?"

I think of the Anthony Tucker who used to snap my bra strap and smell my hair, and I get a lump in my throat. He's changed a lot since I started getting to know him. He even talks about poetry club in the hallways now.

"He's okay," I say, and study his face for a reaction to hearing my voice. His eyebrows disappear under his hair, but I can tell he's working to keep his expression calm.

"Good," he says, a slow smile creeping across his face. "Good, I'm really glad."

I smile back at him. "Hey . . . thanks for the . . . you know."

"No, I don't know."

"The poetry."

He laughs. "I mean, I didn't *invent* it . . ."

"No, but you wrote that note in my . . . in my notebook about sending my poems in, and . . . just, thanks, okay?"

He's still grinning. "You're welcome. Hey. That reminds me. The prize list for the August contest is in, and we did *not* kick butt. Which means I need something amazing from you ASAP. Like, yesterday, if you can swing it. The deadline's the end of November, and they announce the prizes in February. We need a win, Sasha! *I* need a win from my poetry club!" He loops an arm around my shoulder and escorts me down the hallway, still talking about how unjust it is that nobody from our junior high has ever won a poetry scholarship. It feels so natural to talk with Anthony again that I don't even notice the other kids in the hallway staring when they hear my voice.

Two weeks past Mikey's homecoming, Hubert Harless owns the cleanest house in the town of Caboose, and I own the emptiest notebook. I don't understand where all my words have gone. In those quiet months when Mikey was missing, I never had trouble writing things down. Words poured out of my pen. Now that Mikey's back, I have my voice again—I remind Mikey to wear a jacket or to eat his cereal or to take a bath—but my poetry has vanished. Six or seven times a day, I pick up my notebook, grip my pen, bend low, determined to write something to give to Anthony. I write a word or two and scratch them out. Write half a sentence and scratch it out. Nothing feels real. I feel like I'm still waiting for something big to happen, and until it does, I won't know what to write.

So I close the notebook. I drop the pen. Then I pick it up again and put it neatly in the pencil cup I've placed on Shirley's computer desk, which we have moved to the living room to use as Mikey's homework desk. I hide the notebook under the couch cushions, where it stays. Then I fluff the cushions. And I fold the quilt and hang it neatly over the back of the couch. And I pick up Mikey's shoes from the rug and set them carefully by the door. And I get out the vacuum for the mud left behind. And before I know it, a whole evening has slipped by and Hubert is stomping in from work and I have coal dust to clean up. Outside, too, there is filth. I scrub every window in the house. The glass is new but already settled with a gray film of coal dust. It settles on everything for miles. I walk outside and stand on my tiptoes. The glass comes clean, sparkles like water. But by morning there's a film on the windows again. The notebook stays hidden. The pen stays in the cup. I have rags and Windex. I do not have words.

I play with Mikey like nothing is wrong. He is ten years old. He needs to play. But I'm relieved, deep down, in secret, when Mikey starts going next door to play with Phoebe. I'm not able to play properly, and Mikey is annoyed with me for hounding him about homework and muddy shoes and not eating enough at dinner. I don't even know why I'm doing these things, but they roll out before I can stop them. Sometimes I sound so much like my brother, Michael, that I wonder if this is how it was for him; if he cared so much, he couldn't help what he was saying. The thought makes me feel better, both about disappointing Michael and about my harping on Mikey. Still, it's good, I think, when he finds someone he likes to play with who won't pester him about the things I can't help pestering him about.

Anyway, he and Phoebe are thick as thieves, building forts out of blankets, pouring chocolate chips into muffins. Phoebe finally starts speaking above a whisper once she starts playing with Mikey. I can hear their voices up and down the block. But at night in our house, he is still quiet. I start to think I've done something wrong to make him this way. We can't find our rhythm. We're awkward and out of sync. And at night, he barely sleeps. He can't stay warm, or he's too hot. At dinner he eats everything, or nothing at all, with no in between.

I keep expecting things to get better, but they don't. And then I figure, maybe they won't get better. Maybe this is just the way things are now.

I'm elbow-deep in dishwater when I feel like somebody's standing in the doorway, and I turn and find Mikey looking at me.

"Sasha," he says, "I'm real sorry."

"What are you sorry for? You're not the one who messed up."

"Yeah, I did. I ran off without you. I let the cops get you."

"It's not like they arrested me; they just gave me to Hubert. Mikey, *I'm* sorry." I cross to him, pulling a dish towel from the oven handle to dry my hands, and stop just shy of him. "I'm really sorry. Hubert was just fine. I didn't . . . I was so scared to find out, but he was *fine*. I shouldn't have made us run away."

"I went with you on purpose," Mikey said. "I didn't want you to run away without me. When you first moved in with Phyllis, Dad told me you was sad and maybe you needed a friend, and I thought if you ran off, you wouldn't have anybody, so I went with you."

The words make my throat close up with tears. While I was dragging Mikey out of town to protect him, he was trying to protect me by playing along. All at once, I've got my arms around him, and he's squeezing me around the middle.

"I was so scared for you," I whisper. "Mikey Harless, don't you scare me like that ever again!"

"Promise," he mumbles into my T-shirt.

Once Mikey goes back out to play, I return to the dishes, standing where Shirley always stood. In Phyllis's window I can see dirty dishes piled high in her sink, and I know she's out on the porch watching Phoebe and Mikey, doing more important things than dishes. I think how Shirley must have felt these last few years, standing here, washing dishes for a man who didn't love her enough. Condensation drips down the inside of my window, and my hair is curling with the dampness. So it takes me some time to realize there are tears running down my cheeks and plopping off my chin.

When the poem hits, I'm so surprised that I drop the mug I'm washing. It breaks, and the pieces disappear in the dishwater, shards to find and deal with later. I scramble so quickly for my pen, I knock the cup off the desk, and pens and pencils scatter and roll. I fall onto the couch and dig for my notebook. I rip open to a blank page, and little bits of paper from the spirals scatter down into the blankets. I'm undoing all the clean that's been keeping me distracted. I have words.

28

I won't speak. Not permanently—just right now, because I'm nervous. So Anthony does. He reads my new poem out loud. His voice rises and falls.

Afterward, he waits. Nobody says anything. For a minute, they're like me.

Lisa adjusts her neckline, which is lower than the dress code technically allows. Jaina is sitting with Lisa and their new friend, Maggie. The other girls pick at their fingernails. I watch Jaina for a minute, and she looks at me. She smiles just a little. I know Jaina tried to be my friend. She tried really hard, but I didn't try back. It's harder with her than with Anthony. Anthony is okay with quiet.

It's Miss Jacks who breaks the silence, shaking her head and letting out a long breath. "Well," she says. "Sasha, welcome back."

• • •

Anthony catches up with me in the hallway with the cracking, sinking linoleum and the smell of old flood. He leans against the lockers, and he looks at me and looks at me.

"Where did it come from?" he asks.

There are so many complicated ways to answer that question. I think about how, for so long, I've tried to figure out a way to balance the inside of my head and the out. Inside my head, there is poetry, and there are memories of Michael and Ben and Judy all the time. There are plans for escape and fears of what will happen if I don't, and a bigger fear that by the time I figure out how to escape, I won't want to anymore.

And outside my head, there are people trying to get to know me. Anthony writing in my notebook and never asking me to speak. Miss Jacks encouraging me to write. All the poetry club kids sharing their words. And at home, Hubert taking me into his family. Mikey doing things the way he thinks I would do them. Phyllis, always meeting me halfway.

"I'm not sure," I say, because there's no way to explain all the thoughts in my head.

29

"I didn't know you entered any contest," Hubert says. A little more than a month has passed since I turned in my poem for the contest. It's January, and we're on the porch, putting down salt because they're calling for snow. Phyllis and Phoebe are sitting on our steps, playing with Stella, who has followed them over.

"I might not win," I remind them. "I have to perform at the conference in February. Then they'll announce the winners."

"You'll win," Phyllis says, with complete confidence. "You have earned this, sweet Sasha."

I kiss her cheek, then scoop Stella up and look her in the eye. "You're not eating all Miss Phoebe's food now, are you?"

Phoebe giggles. "She begs for everything. She's like a dog."

"More like one than Chip," I agree. "He's like a . . . like a bearskin rug. Unless you've got a stick."

"So where is this conference?" Hubert asks.

"Charleston."

"And when do we go?"

"It's the second week in February." I like how he used the word *do*, like we're definitely going to do it.

"And you get to read your poem to everybody?"

I nod. Hubert nods, too, and tugs at his scrub-brush beard. "Well, little lady, I can't wait to hear it," he says.

30

We drive up the road, up the mountain, up the state. Trailers grow into houses and houses thicken into businesses and people grow into cleaner and gentler and more polite people.

Being free of Caboose, watching places change outside the windows, makes me feel like I'll put a foot wrong, put a word wrong, trip and fall in front of everybody, and I won't even know how to land properly. I'll skin my elbows when a normal girl would have skinned her knees.

The weather is that perfect mix of sun and snow, with frost still sketched on the windshields of parked cars. We're only going for a day, but I feel giddy with travel and achy with homesick, and there is a pain I can't find the word for, which has something to do with how badly I want to win this contest, with its built-in gift of eventual escape, just the way Michael wanted. And, also, how badly I don't want to win, because if I win a scholarship, I don't have a good excuse for not leaving Caboose someday— and Caboose is where my people are.

I can barely remember the hustle and bustle of Beckley. I can barely remember wanting to be a part of it. Charleston is something else again. In Charleston there are tall buildings like you'd expect to find in a city, but the mountains are taller, too. The whole place is tucked into the crook of the mountains. I think of how every state in the nation has a nickname. How ours is the "Mountain State." I've always hated that name. Our mountains, down Caboose way, make me carsick. They're not majestic with their strip-mining bald spots. They look injured.

These mountains are different. They complete the city. They're something special.

The buildings, too. There is nothing like them down our way. Some are golden. Some shine like mirrors.

This day is something special. Maybe I'll shine, too.

I almost chicken out, but then Hubert finds me backstage. The director of the poetry conference looks so relieved to see Hubert that I almost laugh.

"What's going on, little lady?" he asks.

"What if I don't win?"

He shakes his head. "Who says you got to win? You

324

won already. You, standing up in front of people, talking." He rests a heavy hand on my shoulder. "I am so happy I get to hear your voice every day. Including today, reading this poem."

"But what—but, Hubert, what if I win?"

He laughs. "Well, that's a good thing, right?"

"I get a scholarship and in a few years I have to go to college and . . . and Mikey will still be a kid. And there's Phyllis . . . and you . . ."

"Sasha. Who says you have to go away?"

I swallow hard on the name, tears welling up. "Michael."

Hubert nods slowly. "Your brother wanted what was best for you."

"Yeah."

"Well, your brother didn't know you was gonna meet all us family, did he? So what's best for you maybe changed since you saw him."

"But I don't want to have to decide without him!" Now the tears spill, but Hubert laughs.

"I get it," he says. "I do. Michael had a plan for you, and it took away the pressure of deciding. But in the end, kid, we all got to make the call by ourselves. You have to do what's right for you."

I remember writing that same thing to Mikey in my poetry notebook, back when he was missing. But it's harder when we're talking about me. "I don't *know* what's right for me!"

"Which is lucky," Hubert says, "because you're fourteen years old. You've got time, Sasha."

"Not much time," the conference director interjects, catching the end of our conversation. "I need you on the stage in five minutes, Miss Harless."

Hubert straightens his button-up. He looks as uncomfortable as Mikey, but Phyllis made them both dress up a bit. He hooks a finger under my chin and lifts it so we're looking at each other.

"You look pretty as a very pretty picture," he says. "And I can't wait to hear what you've written." He kisses me on the forehead and makes his way back down the stage stairs and out of sight. But I don't feel alone. I feel like he's still standing there next to me.

I take my seat in the white plastic chair and study the shiny wooden stage floor under my feat. I shift and then shift again to make sure my dress is covering all the right parts of me. I try to hold my paper still, but it shakes in my nervous hands, too flimsy for the weight of all the words.

The kids on the stage with me are clutching flimsy sheets of printer paper, too. All around me, 8½" x 11" rectangles of white, nervous words tremble under the stage lights. There are so many kids about to step up and read their innermost thoughts. At least one other rectangle of truth must be something like mine.

Until now, I've been focused on my own flimsy white

paper. On my own shaky words. Now I realize that I'm glad I came. I can't wait to hear what is in these other heads.

We sit behind the guest speaker, who is not really speaking to us. Down in the crowd, out of sight in the dark, our parents and guardians murmur and rustle. I can't see Hubert in the crowd. I can't see Phyllis or Phoebe. I can't see Mikey, but I know he's next to Phoebe and I know he's giggling with excitement from the road trip. I can't see Anthony.

I hope there's an empty chair somewhere in the crowd, holding a spot for my big brother, Michael, or my father, Ben. If there had been no fire at the Cupcake Emporium, maybe that chair would be filled. If the Hardwater mine had never fallen in, maybe that chair would be filled. But too many things have happened for maybe.

The speaker talks about how we have our futures in front of us, and our stories are only beginning. We can write them any way we want. We can develop a solid plot. We can choose our supporting characters with care. We can every one of us arrive at the final chapter with a happy ending.

But this contest was for poetry, not prose. I think his metaphor isn't quite right.

The dean of the college steps up and clears her throat.

She explains about the prize money and the scholarships. I think about college. I think about how, if I win, or even if I don't, maybe I will choose *this* college. I look at my blurred reflection, a haze of color on the freshly waxed floor. I look different. Older. For the first time in a long time, I don't feel like I'm from someplace bad. If I can write poetry back home that gets me the chance to step under these stage lights, then maybe I'll be okay. Maybe I can hang on long enough to grow into the girl Michael wanted me to be. Or even the girl *I* want to be.

There are so many people on the stage and in the audience. They expect me to stand at the microphone. They expect me to open my mouth, which has been quiet too often in the year since Michael died, and let a poem come out.

"My name is Sasha Harless." I can barely pronounce it. I'm nervous. My voice is shaky like moth wings. "I'm in the eighth grade. I'm fourteen." This is the information everyone volunteered. Their name. Their age. Now is where it gets different. I've heard so many beautiful poems tonight, all about kids doing things they want to do. So many of the poetry forms Anthony and the club taught me have been read tonight. I've heard haiku, short and sweet. I've heard epistles pleading with family members. I've heard tanka all about the beauty of snow.

I try three times to say the word *we*.

The first time, I'm too close to the microphone. I startle back, and there's a low rumble of laughter down in the invisible audience.

The second time, my voice just plain doesn't work. I open my mouth and nothing comes out, and the sensation is so familiar it's almost comforting. Then I think of Mikey's mother by the road, green smudge at her throat, talking and talking but not saying anything. I close my mouth, get one more run at it. Open it. Begin.

We—
all of us folks from there—
will meet again someday,
driving down and down
on winding roads
we aren't used to anymore,
when we're grown.

Our wives, husbands, children
will gasp with fear.
They have never seen roads like this.

They will stare
at the crumbles of buildings,
at the crumbles of roads,
at the crumbles of generations
gone before,

and they will be amazed
that we ever made it out
with our sanity and our humor
and our lives and our words.
But I have a confession.

When I think of leaving
the place where I was born,
the place where I have passed
each miserable, no-good day—
each hopeful, got-to-get-better day—
each rare, peaceful, lying-in-the-sunshine day—

I lose all my words,
just for a minute,
and pictures fill me and fill me up.

Me and my cousin
on the front porch on our backs
with the sun pouring down in buckets.

And
a kind neighbor in a kitchen
teaching us to preheat, to grease the pan,
to step lightly so the cake won't fall.
Common sense, *she says.*

She doesn't know how
uncommon she is.

And fog
heavy on
morning mountains
that don't know any better
than to be beautiful
even above the coal slurry
and the fast cars crashing
and the coal mines caving
and the bedsheets waving,
God bless these lost miners,
God keep these lost miners,
in bloodred, hopeless spray paint
from a now-empty can.

I am shocked to realize that
today I am homesick
for a place I never even knew I loved.

The paper stops trembling halfway through, and when I finish, there is silence—half a second of quiet so deep it might as well be written in my poetry notebook. Then there is clapping and, under the clapping, murmuring, and I hear one lady—it might be Phyllis—say, "Oh!"

Then the stage lights dim in between readers, and my eyes single out a familiar, coal-miner-shaped shadow in the crowd, and love pours into me like water into a glass, and my tears spill over, and I know, without being able to see, that Hubert has tears on his cheeks, too, because we're family, and family knows.

31

Hours later, while Hubert shakes off the cold and walks toward his daughters' bedroom out of habit, then steers toward his own instead, Mikey and me sit on the couch, which has not yet warmed. Even the crocheted blanket off the back of the couch is cold. The baseboard heaters tick and stutter and push out a skinny beam of lukewarm air. Mikey drapes sideways so he can press his bare feet against the heater. There is a messy pile of shoes by the door: dirty gray sneakers and one yellow sandal, left-behind high heels and coal-black work boots. I haven't yet kicked off the simple gray dress and shoes Phyllis picked out for me at the pawnshop. Once I take them off, the trip is over. I reach into my pocket to touch the check, my prize money for second place. It will be enough to replace a GUI-tar so Phyllis can sing to Phoebe. It will be enough to make one thing right.

"Sasha?" Mikey asks, his voice heavy with sleep, although he insisted all the way home that he would rather be on a road trip than in bed any day. Today he wants to be a truck driver. He wants to haul something fun, like chickens or carnival rides, but if he drives a truck around here, I know what he'll haul. The roads and our families have chipped away under the weight of it. I've told him he won't be choosing that career. That he'll go to college and learn to do something safe. He laughed me off. I'm his cousin. I'm not a parent, not a guardian. I cannot tell him what to do.

I look at him slowly because I feel like something is different in his voice, and I'm tired, too, and I'm sunk in a fog of half happy from the travel and the winning, and half ready to cry, with relief and dismay, that we've come home.

"Where you think you'll go with that scholarship?" he asks. There is a hitch of sad. But college is a hundred years in the future. He knows I won't be leaving yet.

I look around the living room. Even in the dark I can see the red of the kitchen. There aren't so many apples now. As I clean, I put more and more of them away. The house is hunkered down for sleep, a different place entirely at night than during the day. Something is missing to make it completely home. I think of how something was missing up Charleston way, too, something I looked for as we walked around town celebrating my victory. Something familiar and comfortable. Something I didn't find. I think of how maybe every place has something missing. Maybe what fills it up and makes it whole is the people there.

I listen to the ticking of the baseboard heater and the groan of frost seizing the window glass and the settling sounds of the house.

"Somewhere," I tell Mikey before I shove him off the couch and aim him toward his bedroom. He's asleep on his feet. He's dreaming of the open road. He doesn't hear the rest of my answer. "I'm going somewhere. You and me both." The darkness swallows up my words, but that's all right. I've got more.

Acknowledgments

I'm grateful to so many people who have helped *Free Verse* become a reality!

Without my agent, Laura Langlie, I would be lost in the tall grass most of the time.

If I told you how patient Stacey Barney and Kate Meltzer at Putnam have been with me, you wouldn't even believe it. It sounds made up, and, after all, I do write fiction. But this time I'm telling the truth.

I'm extraordinarily grateful to Phyllis Reynolds Naylor, Daniel Handler, Lyn Miller-Lachmann, Neal Shusterman, Susanna Reich, and the PEN American Center for their faith in me and in *Free Verse* in awarding me the PEN/ Phyllis Naylor Working Writer Fellowship in 2012. With their help, I was able to devote the time and energy to the novel to bring it into the light.

While I was working on this novel, I was also leading a weekly youth writing group at Cabell County Public Library. My library writers—talented, devoted kids who showed up faithfully to the library each week to dazzle me with their characters, stories, and energy—gave Sasha her poetry club and gave me the inspiration to complete *Free Verse*. I am grateful to, and remain in awe of, Beth Anne, Elaine, Matthew, Abby, Darius, Chloe, Lauren, Jasmine, Alice, Aaron, and so many other writers who shared their work with us over the years. I can't wait to hold your books in my hands.

I'm so grateful to early readers Sheila and Cassie for taking time away from their own full plates to offer advice on early drafts. I must also thank Janell Reynolds and her son Jamie for the time they spent squinting into the sun to capture an author photo. And I'm forever indebted to Curtis and his momma, Melissa, for making me put down the book and get some fresh air once in a while!

I don't know where I would be without the support and encouragement of my Bright Futures work family. When I traveled to NYC to accept the award from PEN, I was wearing an outfit from Jill's own closet, which Teri helped me choose. Bev, who can materialize anything from nothing, supplied matching handbags. Alexis created an amazing city skyline banner, which hangs in my writing space to this day, and the lot of them saw me off with a reminder not to be so nervous, that it was enough to be myself—something I do better in their company than almost any other time.

I walked into the shadows to write parts of this novel, and Jake Lilly held the light so I could find my way back. Thanks for that, friend.

Free Verse wouldn't exist if not for my parents, Mark and Kate, and my sisters, Jennifer and Heather. I'm also convinced that Maria Lynette Goodyear and Emmett Isaac Lynch are my good-luck charms.

Keep reading for a sneak peek
of the next book!

*ashes to
asheville*

chapter
1

Right before my sister, Zany, steals
our dead mother off the mantel, I'm trying to decide
which sock to stuff in Haberdashery's mouth to shut
him up. He's barking every five seconds, *yip yip yip*, all
shrill like a smoke detector with its batteries low. It's
a wonder Mrs. Madison hasn't come downstairs in her
slippery cheetah robe, waving Mr. Madison's ancient
handgun. She keeps the thing in her purse, says a widow
as pretty as her needs protection, especially with, what
she calls it, her *assets*. I thought she was talking dirty the
first time I heard that, till Mama Shannon explained she
meant money.

Before Zany reaches for the mantel, my biggest
problem is whether to sacrifice my left sock, which is

blue and belongs to Mama Shannon, or my right sock, which is purple and was Mama Lacy's. I miss both my mamas. I don't want to give up either of their socks, but how else am I going to shut this dog up before Mrs. Madison wakes to find that my sister's broken in?

I've pretty much decided on Mama Shannon's sock, both because Mama Shannon is alive to wear other socks and because I'm a little bit mad at her, even though I don't want to be. When Zany reaches for the mantel, I'm still holding the blue sock in my left hand, all foot-shaped and the bottom covered with Haberdashery hair. But I'm not still thinking about the yipping dog, although he's in a tizzy now that the midnight intruder has proven to be a thief.

"We're not supposed to touch that!" My whisper falls in between Haberdashery's yips, and it's loud as sandpaper on splintery wood.

Zany eases Mama Lacy's curvy brass container down off the mantel and clutches it to her chest. I call it a cookie jar, because I don't like the word *urn*. I can see it rising and falling with her uneven breath. Even in the half dark, I can make out the smile across her lips. Grinning and breathing hard and doing something crazy, that's why Zany gets called Zany instead of Zoey Grace and that's why she's not supposed to drink more than half a Mountain Dew per day. But this might be the craziest thing she's ever done.

"Mama Shannon says only followers do what they're 'supposed to,'" she whispers, "and Culvert women are born leaders. Come on." She starts for the door, and I follow her, even though I know Mrs. Madison is going to freak out if she wakes up and Mama Lacy and I are both gone. I follow her, even though Haberdashery panics when he sees the door swing open, and starts tugging on my remaining sock. I wonder whether Madison women are born followers, because the truth is, all I ever do is follow Zany. She always knows the way.

The night air is a shock to my system. That's what Mama Lacy would have called it: "a shock to the system." Mama Shannon would say it was "colder than a witch's toe." Or a witch's something else if she thought we kids weren't close enough to hear. Mama Lacy and Mama Shannon couldn't have been more different in how they talked. They were so different, I thought it was a wonder they ever managed to fall in love.

After living with Mrs. Madison for months, it's easy for me to understand why Mama Lacy always talked so fancy. There are entire sentences Mrs. Madison says that I don't understand. Stuff like, "Kindly escort me to the sitting room," or, "Be a dear and please grant me the pleasure of your company at the breakfast table." Stuff that would make more sense if she didn't clutter it up with all that fancy talk.

The brass jar is glinting in the weak light, and I follow it through the darkness. It's cold enough to steal your breath. It's still February for one more day, and Zany didn't exactly give me time to change when she committed *Grand Theft Mother*. I'm dressed in a slippery bubblegum-pink robe Mrs. Madison bought me over my flannel PJ pants and a yellow Milk Duds T-shirt that belongs to Mama Shannon. I'm still only wearing one sad purple sock.

Zany isn't dressed much warmer, but hers is on purpose. Low-cut tank top, tight-fitting jeans, clunky boots, and a sweater that looks like it's made to show off the tank top, not to actually keep a body warm. Still, when Zany sees me shiver, she pulls off the sweater and swings it around me, and it's cozy from her arms. I hold it close and I feel the oddest thing, since Zany is right here in front of me. I feel homesick for her, the same way I feel for Mama Shannon, who I hardly ever get to see, and for Mama Lacy, who I won't ever see again. My feet stumble to catch up to my sister. I don't hold her hand, because I'm twelve, but I wish I could.

At the end of the drive is Mama Shannon's car, and that's when I know this isn't going to be any quick thing.

I don't know how I thought Zany got here. I guess I didn't think about it. I'm not so good with the details. Mama Lacy was always smoothing my hair and telling me, "You can focus better, Fella. I know you can." Mama Shannon's wording was a little less delicate: "If you tripped over a dead body on the floor, you'd say 'pardon me' and keep right on walking." Which might be true—there was that time I said "Excuse me" to the parking meter when I bumped into it with my elbow and I thought it was a person—but I don't like having it pointed out. It's not that I don't try to pay attention. It's just that there are so many things to pay attention *to*.

"Where we going?" I ask.

"Remember the ice creams, Fella?" Zany changes the subject as she unlocks the car doors. I think it was pretty responsible of her to remember to lock them. I have no idea what she's babbling about, all I know is that the seats are freezing when I try to sit, and I don't want to think about ice cream right now.

"What ice creams?"

"The ice cream bars at Mack and Morello's."

I lower my butt to the seat, then hitch it back into the air. Still too cold.

"I remember Mack and Morello's, but I don't think I remember ice cream bars."

5

Zany pauses with her hand at the ignition and gazes past me for a minute. I wish she'd turn the key so the heat would come on. I'm getting tired of hovering above the seat. "They had two flavors, Heath bar and strawberry shortcake. I liked strawberry shortcake because it was pink, and you liked Heath bar because it wasn't." She turns the key at last. I like how Mama Shannon's car engine sounds. It's rough and warm. It's got a different voice than other cars. I hear it and I hear Mama Shannon's own voice, talking up in front while I'm dozing in the back. I miss her so much.

"No, I don't remember that." I don't mean to sound annoyed, but I do anyway. Zany is sixteen, so she's got four years more memories than me. But even the memories we share, she remembers better. I remember what the purple door sounded like at Mack and Morello's, the way the bell jingled extra loud if I came in at a run. I remember an orange floor and something about dropping a hot dog.

"Why are you thinking about Mack and Morello's?" I ask.

"You know your seat's never going to get warm if you don't put your butt on it."

"Yuh-huh, the heat will warm it up."

"Yeah, maybe by the time we get there. Nothing in

this car works all the way like it's supposed to." Zany puts the car in reverse and starts down the driveway. She twists to look over her shoulder and I twist to look at her.

"Get where?" I latch on to the important part of her words.

But she ignores the question. "Put on your seat belt."

I turn to reach for my seat belt, and I catch a glimpse of something moving in the darkness outside the car. Something fast and familiar and extremely pesky.

"Wait!" I roll down my window and hear yipping.

Zany hits the brakes. "How'd that dumb thing get out?"

"He must have run out when we left. He's always doing that. Zany, I have to take him back!"

Zany studies the upstairs windows, still and dark. "You can't do that. He's too loud. And anyways it's always when thieves go back that they get caught." I'm surprised she owns up to being a thief. Then I realize she's including me.

"We can't steal him, too," I protest.

"It's not stealing. We'll be back before anyone's awake."

My hopes fall. I guess I sort of thought Zany was here to steal me.

The view from the front is different from where I usually ride in the back. I slowly lower my rear end to the cold seat, and I open the door and let Haberdashery in. He yips approval and climbs into the back, where he immediately gets to work making the seat comfortable by pawing at the fabric.

Zany backs down the driveway again, and I feel a little panicky at the thought of doing something as big as running away, and then coming back at dawn and getting caught. What if Mrs. Madison catches me sneaking Mama Lacy's ashes onto the mantel? Zany is cradling the brass jar in the crook of one elbow while she steers with her free arm. I ought to reach over and take Mama Lacy before she gets dropped, but I can't make my arms move. I've never held my mother's remains before and I don't plan to start now.

Zany puts the car in drive and we start down the darkened street. Even though I'm certain we're either going to go to jail or get in trouble with Mrs. Madison— and I am not sure which is worse—I feel a thick excitement at passing the MADISON DRIVE sign. Mrs. Madison isn't the only person who lives on Madison Drive, but hers was the first house here and remains the biggest. As far as I understand it, the city had to name the street after my great-grandfather to convince him to sell his lawn for development. I haven't been off this block in months, unless it was in a school bus or on our tense visits to church. Even though there's a shiny gold car in her garage, Mrs. Madison doesn't drive. Twice a year, a man comes to take the car to the mechanic for a checkup. I don't see the point, since that man is the only person who ever gets behind the wheel, but Mrs. Madison says a lady must take responsibility for her vehicle. She sounds about a thousand years old when she says it, and Mama Shannon always rolls her eyes if she's there. If she's not, that's when Mrs. Madison starts muttering about "that woman" Mama Lacy took up with, who lets her tires run down to the cable before she ever buys new ones.

"That woman" is Mrs. Madison's name for Mama Shannon. And it's true. Mama Shannon does let the tires run down to the cable. She also forgets to do things like get oil changes until the sticker on the windshield says she's late by at least a whole month. And her glove box is full of tickets—for parking, for speeding, for forgetting to put the right stickers on the outside of the car. She and I are a lot alike in that way. It used to drive Mama Lacy crazy how forgetful me and Mama Shannon could be.

Still, I don't see that it's Mrs. Madison's business how Mama Shannon treats her car. So I'm happy to get off Madison Drive, but my stomach is in knots because

I also don't want to get in trouble. I still haven't gotten in real, huge trouble at the Madison house and I don't know what will happen. Will I get lectured? Ignored? Sent to bed without supper? Mrs. Madison seems formal enough that she could probably write me a ticket or send me to detention or something. Or maybe she hides what Mama Lacy called "a volatile heart" beneath that slippery cheetah robe and she'll get mad and yell and scream at me. My stomach feels wilty at the thought.

"Zany, I don't think we should be doing this." My excitement tips back over into panic.

Zany rolls her eyes. "You always say that about everything. And you're too late. We're already doing it." She spins the wheel at the corner and juggles her armload of urn, at last pushing it toward me. I try not to take it, but Zany lets go. If I don't catch it, it'll fall. It sinks into my palms, heavier than I thought it would be. It's almost as heavy as one of the weights Mama Shannon uses when she's stair-stepping.

Zany hits the gas once we get out on the main road. She turns on the radio, cranks the volume, and sings along to a tune that sounds as pink as my robe, all about falling in love. Gross. I clutch my dead mother to my chest, all cold and brass, as we escape through the night.

chapter
2

There's a picture on the dashboard of a perfect family: two parents and two kids, all girls. It was taken in 1999, the year we moved back to West Virginia from Asheville. You can't tell by looking, because our eyes are full of smiles, but already it was the beginning of the end of good things for us. Five years have passed since then, and not a single one has been easy.

We loved Asheville. I might be the youngest person in the family and have the poorest memory, but our love for our home, I'll never forget that. It wasn't just something we felt. It was something we talked about. Mama Shannon was always going on about how back home in West Virginia, she couldn't do this and back home she couldn't do that. But in North Carolina, in Asheville, she could do and be and say whatever she wanted, and nobody would get upset with her for it. She wore cargo shorts from the men's section and got her hair cut at the barbershop and she talked openly with anyone who asked about her love for Mama Lacy and the city they'd chosen.

Mama Lacy's love wasn't as loud. But she used to watch Mama Shannon with a smile on her lips. She used to nod at the right places in Mama Shannon's sto-ries—"Back home, we couldn't find a church that ac-cepted us as a lesbian couple." *Nod.* "Back home, we didn't want to send the kids to school knowing they were going to get teased for having two mothers." *Nod.*

Zany used to nod, too, seriously, as though she un-derstood. Maybe she did. Zany was old enough to re-member moving *to* Asheville, not just *from.* We moved to the city in 1994 when she was a first grader after Mama Lacy and Mama Shannon realized our neighbors in West Virginia weren't ever going to like us.

In Asheville, our family was accepted. Though it wasn't legal there or anywhere else for my parents to be married, there were more gay people in the area and it was more accepted for them to raise kids and have fami-lies together. We were able to go to school there without much fuss—I remember a couple of dumb kids picking on me about my moms, but those were the same kids

12

who picked on me about my tangled hair or my oversize rain boots that I'd stolen from Zany. And there were some substitute teachers who had a little trouble understanding. Overall, though, Asheville was kind to us.

Still, in between figuring out what they wanted to be when they grew up—something neither of my moms ever settled on—and going about their daily lives of squabbling and laughing and mopping floors and fixing dinner, my parents watched the news with hope.

"It's coming," Mama Shannon used to say when something good would happen in the news. When civil unions became legal in Vermont, when a politician would mention gay marriage during a debate, when other countries legalized it, Mama Shannon would get so excited she couldn't hold still. She would work harder on whatever project held her fancy at the moment—building footstools out of driftwood, sanding old chairs to make them look new again. "Picture it, Lacy! *Real* marriage is coming!"

I didn't like when she brought up those things, because it meant pointing out that the marriage they already had wasn't a real marriage. It sure *looked* real, just like the marriages on TV. They hugged and they fought and they danced and they kissed and sometimes Mama Shannon slept on the couch and sometimes Mama Lacy washed the same dish six or seven times while thundering under her breath, "Shannon's too daggone old to play guitar in a band" or, "Can't Shannon even see when there's no toilet paper on the roll? It wouldn't kill her to change it."

Sometimes they even fought about their wedding.

"I'm not getting married in a church, Lace."

"That's where weddings happen."

"Weddings happen all kinds of places."

"Well, *my* wedding will be happening in a church, so if you'd like to be one of the brides, you can waltz your happy butt into the church and act civilized for five minutes."

Mama Shannon grimaced. "Bride? I'm a bride?"

"What would you rather be? You're not a groom, are you? I never meant to get one of those." Mama Lacy bit the tip of her tongue the way she did when she was teasing. "I can think of some other names to call you. Which do you prefer?"

"I don't know." Mama Shannon was laughing now, too. "I'm your partner. I'm your . . . your significant other."

" 'You may now kiss the significant other'? That lacks the ring of romance, babe."

"Fine. Wife. We're wives. 'Bride' just sounds so . . . young." Mama Shannon leaned in toward Mama Lacy.

"I mean, *you* can be a bride. You're still young and beautiful. You can pass this old ogre off as your spouse, but you can't convince me I'm a 'bride.'"

They had dozens of conversations like this, and at the end, Mama Lacy would lean in to kiss Mama Shannon's hand or cheek or lips, and then Zany and I squealed that they were gross and would they please knock it off because there were children in the room. And they would break apart and pillow-fight us or tickle us until we thought we were going to pee, but Mama Shannon would always come back to the way things were finally starting to change.

"It's really going to happen," she would say. "We're going to be spouses, brides, whatever, in this lifetime."

Except you never really know how long a lifetime's going to be.

When Mama Lacy got sick with pancreatic cancer, we stayed in Asheville for a while. But soon, she wasn't able to work. It was cheaper to live in West Virginia, and Mama Lacy and Mama Shannon both had family here who could help with things like cleaning the house and watching us kids. The family wasn't perfect. Mostly, Mrs. Madison took me while Mama Shannon's mama,

Granny Culvert, who lived close by back then, watched Zany and helped with the house.

I remember being happy with Mrs. Madison in those days. Being in a family with a big sister with such a giant personality, it was fun to be spirited away and have all the attention on me for a while. Mrs. Madison taught me how to play games I was too young for, like bridge and poker. She taught me how to make snow angels, and peanut butter sandwiches with Marshmallow Fluff. At the end of each day, she used to wrap me up in one of her robes and plunk me on the sofa with iced tea if it was warm out, hot cocoa if it wasn't, and we would watch her game shows together. We were so cozy, I called her Grandma once or twice, though it never quite felt as natural as calling her Mrs. Madison the way everybody else did. She always glowed with pride when I could answer the questions on the TV before the contestants. Any time we met any of her friends out at the store, she would brag to them about the most recent thing I'd known that she didn't think a kid my age would. She was usually wrong—all the kids at school could do the same things I could do, and sometimes, more—but I never corrected her. I liked her to think I was special.